H.A. e

W9-DBI-448

GREED AT GOLD RIVER

LAURAN PAINE

GREED AT GOLD RIVER

Thorndike Press • Chivers Press
Thorndike, Maine USA   Bath, Avon, England

This Large Print edition is published by Thorndike Press, USA and by Chivers Press, England.

Published in 1994 in the U.S. by arrangement with Golden West Literary Agency.

Published in 1994 in the U.K. by arrangement with the author.

U.S. Hardcover   0-7862-0257-2   (Western Series Edition)
U.K. Hardcover   0-7451-2621-9   (Chivers Large Print)
U.K. Softcover   0-7451-2622-7   (Camden Large Print)

The text of this Large Print edition is unabridged.
Other aspects of the book may vary from the original edition.

Set in 16 pt. News Plantin by Barbara Ingerson.

Printed in the United States on acid-free paper.

British Library Cataloguing in Publication Data available

Library of Congress Cataloging in Publication Data

Paine, Lauran.
    Greed at Gold River / Lauran Paine.
        p.   cm.
    ISBN 0-7862-0257-2 (alk. paper : lg. print)
    PS3566.A34G7   1994
    813'.54—dc20   94-11176

GREED AT GOLD RIVER

During the period of gold discovery in the American West, the government recognised the needs of the miners and passed legislation that enabled branch mints to be established, or private citizens, in certain cases, to strike coins on crude hand presses. Frequently arguments arose over true weights, fineness of gold and quality of the dust itself. The expedient of using a three-fingered "pinch" to measure quantity was eventually discarded because bartenders were hired for the size of their hands, not ability.

In an effort to create a fictional novel, it has become necessary to invent names of certain towns and people, but the technical aspects of this story can be found in any comprehensive history of the American West today. It is a matter of record, for example, that on February 16th, 1849, the legislature passed a resolution providing that Oregon City, then the largest town in Oregon Territory with a population in excess of one thousand, be permitted to open a branch mint.

This action came late, however. Prior to this time there was near anarchy over the right and need of Oregonians for acceptable currency. It is during this little known epoch of Western history, prior to 1849, that *Greed at Gold River* has its setting.

LAURAN PAINE.

CHAPTER ONE

Divide to Conquer

Cleve Simpson sat relaxed against the rolling motion of the stagecoach, watching Gold River come at him across the tangle of forested undergrowth and slashed-out clearings. His tanned flesh was puckered a little around the grey eyes, the colour of woodsmoke on an overcast day, and the set of his mouth was pensive. He kept his vigil unaware of the veiled but interested look on the black-eyed woman's face who rode diagonally across from him beside her thick barrelled husband.

Neila Willis was a stunning woman with the feline abundance of a ripe tigress. The men at Gold River used her as a measure of something they wanted, but never within earshot of Harold Willis; for aside from owning the Gold River House, combination hotel and saloon, Willis was a man of power in the squalid clutch of shacks that clung to the edge of Clark's River, Oregon Territory.

Cleve knew the Willises were on the stage, but he hadn't looked their way once since leaving the capital. It was a strange situation at that, for there was no open and avowed warfare at all. Still, Harold Willis was the opposition to what Cleve and his miners' committee were trying to do, and both recognised in the other their enemy.

Gold River came up slowly, the last half mile. The stage slowed to walk and jounced over the roadway from the southern entrance to town, letting the horses blow.

Harold Willis raked over the town once with his cold eyes, then flashed a look at Cleve Simpson and relaxed, fishing for a Havana cigar and allowing a little of the hidden scorn and contempt within him to show in the lines around his eyes.

Cleve saw his own shack on the river side of the plankwalk that ended just beyond his front door. It had a deserted look. Then Gold River proper came up to them and the crudeness of it made Cleve wince. The town had arisen in days and weeks when the word of old John Lenthall's fabulous strike in the silt of the river had trickled into the tiring California gold fields. Old John and his shack had been swept away by the horde of newcomers; he had kept his vigil too long. With his murder, Cleve Simpson's first resentment found its voice. He had roared for law, and the others, who were thoughtful men, agreed, and combined their efforts to have an election. The result had been something they had never suspected; Harold Willis had come out at the last minute, sponsoring a man he had imported from Kansas, Ben Carter, and his man was swept into office in a stunning upset that was handled very cleverly by Willis, whose past victories were evident in the manner he handled the present lightning campaign.

Cleve saw the members of his committee waiting expectantly on the duckboards. His mouth got flatter and the sombre look in his eyes was rimmed in pain. He had taken the trip to the capital to condemn the nightly violence that had increased at Gold River. It had increased instead of diminished after Willis's man was elected sheriff; Willis, who found out some way what he was up to, had again beaten him by arriving in the capital one day ahead of him.

"Cleve, boy; what news?"

The stage door was scarcely opened before the men shouted at him. Cleve said nothing, shrugging; then the men saw Neila and Harold Willis step down. It was a general look of astonishment that spread over the rough faces. Gradually then, understanding came, and with it the same bitter, hard look of dogged resolution. They had their answer before Cleve said a word, from the way it showed, not only

9

on Cleve's features, but in the way Harold Willis's eyes shined his triumph without actually smiling.

Cleve stood back and let the Willises go past. His face was blank with appraisal; then Neila's head turned slightly and their eyes met. Her obsidian black ones and the grey, pensive eyes of Cleve Simpson. The look was more one of interest on her part than disinterest on his. Neila's face showed the smallest of smiles that scarcely hovered at the outer corners of her full mouth and the look in her eyes was the same saturnine challenge that showed so often in her husband's glance.

It was something else that Cleve couldn't analyse; part curiosity, no doubt, and part this other thing he had never seen in a woman's eyes before. Then she was gone, swallowed up by the little group of men who crowded around him, waiting.

Cleve shrugged. "You've guessed it, boys; Willis was there a full day ahead of me. He'd had his say. I got sympathy, and that's all."

There was a short silence. Discouragement showed here and there like a blight. This was the miners' committee's second outright defeat. Uncertainty showed, too. Willis was powerful, but so far he had been content to discourage them without showing anything more menacing than contempt for their efforts to create decency where the reign of terror existed. But he might change, and life in Gold River was precarious enough without Willis's wrath. The men shifted on their booted feet and looked at one another, then back at Cleve.

One of the men in the group nodded slowly and raised his eyes to Simpson's face. "Cleve, you look used up. Get some rest. We'll talk this over tonight at the mass meeting. All right?"

Cleve nodded. He felt more beaten than weary, but the tiring, slamming ride over the undulating, rutted roads had made him ache, too. He nodded in silence and went through the men to the plankwalk, stepped up and turned north toward his shack. Ben Carter was standing against the slat-and-bat siding of a store looking at him. Cleve's eyes crossed with the sheriff's hooded stare; neither man nodded, but recognition was there. Then Cleve's sturdy figure, a little hunched, went on past and Ben Carter's gaze followed him coldly, appraisingly.

Ben's appreciation for the rugged, thick body of Cleve Simpson was reluctantly tinged with admiration. Ben, a lanky, thin man well above six feet, carried no flesh to give depth to his height. Cleve, at six feet and an axe handle across the shoulders in width, was a formidable adversary to Ben Carter.

11

Ben watched the miners shuffle back toward their diggings and shoved off the store front, heading toward the Gold River House. Willis's trip to the capital affected him as sheriff and he wanted to know who had won out, although there wasn't much trepidation in Carter.

Inside the Gold River House was a cross section of the community; a glimpse of the avalanche of miners that had clumped into the wilderness where old John Lenthall's shack had been and ground the earth into dust, making the serene Utopia a bedlam of discord and ruthless determination to tear away the obstacles to wealth that nature had accumulated over the eons in Gold River. Men clawed at the water by day under the humid sunblast of summer and made the surrounding country ring with their savagery by night, finding a moment now and then to erect their shanty town that had been called by common consent and indifference Gold River.

The frenzied wildness of Gold River drew others beside miners; dreamers and outlaws and speculators and merchants, and a few women. At first these were Siwash squaws, dumpy, usually dirty and flat-faced, with morals assuaged by gut-curdling whisky and bits of gold. Later, Mexican women from the upper California camps had drifted in, along with their sisters, the Chileños, and Gold River had come of age. There was a log café that had sprung up out of necessity; a funeral parlour and doctor's shack born of indifference and occasional need; the big log and mud-wattle Gold River House, a saloon and gaming place, mothered of frontier custom and insistence.

Willis's eyes shone dully, like fish scales under water, and Ben Carter sat patiently waiting. "Ben, I seen a lot of new towns along the rivers. Gold River's the best; it'll last. She's going to be a rich town."

"Yes," Carter said, "I know." He had been through this conversation too many times already. Everyone said the same thing, but Ben was a sceptic. He knew how long these gold towns lasted; just as long as the gold, and nothing else could keep them alive. He watched Willis go towards a bottle on a slab table, pour two drinks and bring one back to him without a glimmer of expression on his face. Carter appreciated Willis's taste; brandy was a rare treat in the Territory.

Harold Willis went back behind his desk and looked thoughtfully at Carter's blank face. Its very blankness was indicative of something seeking for a way out. He reached up and flicked perspiration out of the folds of his neck. "I expect you're wondering how I made out?" Willis's eyes crinkled a little. "Good, Ben;

plenty good. The capital men say as long as you're the duly elected sheriff of the countryside, your word is law. To tell you the truth, they really don't care too much about gold towns. They bristle when you mention what you want. There's too many towns now, and more springing up every day. It's the same old story; the Territory's grown faster than the government can keep up with it." Willis smiled a little, lopsidedly. "We're safe enough."

"Willis," Carter said flatly, "there's talk now of electing a damned town marshal."

Willis eased back in his chair and shifted his bulk a little. "That so? They won't give up, huh?" He watched the worry move into Carter's blue eyes.

"And that damned committee; listen, why don't we just knock them out of the way?"

Willis sucked at some strands of his handsome moustache, eyeing his sheriff steadily. "The way these miners are, they'll follow anyone who promises anything." He flicked his hand at a blue-tailed fly near his face. "I've seen it before. It's always the same; a few bags of gold and they start demanding reforms."

Carter nodded. "It ain't too good, Harold."

"Worried, Ben? I don't like this talk about a town marshal because that means someone's trying to clean up Gold River. Besides, you can't ever tell who they'll run for marshal. But I don't see anything to worry about — not yet."

"Well —"

"I've seen some good set-ups spoiled," Willis went on evenly, "by some dreamer being elected to an office so's he can reform a gold camp and stop the very damned things that attracted him there in the first place."

Carter nodded slowly. "That's what I don't like — reforms."

"You sweat too easy, Ben. Nothing to worry about yet. There never will be, either, if we watch them close." Willis watched Carter's face, saw no assurance reflected there, and went on again: "Let it go for now, Ben. The capital boys are behind us. Anyway, there's nothing to be done until they get set, like last time — if they ever do. It'll be easy to bust 'em when we know what we're fighting. You'll see."

"But suppose they do set up a town marshal; hell, Gold River's good pickings."

"Suppose, hell," Willis came out of his chair impatiently. "You've seen this happen before, Ben. Reform movements hit every town once in a while. Sure, they're dangerous; but it depends on the men who fight them whether they succeed or not. Naturally, our set-up is the first one the miners'd go after. We've got

15

to stand that risk because we're the ones who stand to gain the most. I'll back you to the limit, Ben, just like always. We're a hard combination to beat, you and I. Find out all about it — who's sparking it and all — and let me know; then we'll decide what to do."

Carter heaved his long frame upright. "All right, I'll see what's going on." He stood looking doubtfully at the short, massive man behind the desk.

"One more thing before you leave, Ben. I got to thinking about this coming in on the stage. There's a lot of gold being taken out of the river. First, they'll want to establish an assay office, if the take-out warrants it. Next, they'll detail U.S. Marshals to keep the peace. We don't want these things to happen."

"Sure not," Carter agreed.

"There's another thing, too; I've just finished a petition to Washington asking for an assay office in Gold River."

Carter blinked his bewilderment. "But you just said an assay office here —"

Willis shook his head vigorously. "I asked for an assay office here on behalf of the better element in town. As spokesman for that group, I requested that the position of Head Assayer be granted to me for this part of Oregon Territory." Willis laughed. "By the time I'm through with Gold River, the Indians can have it back, and they'll be welcome to it."

Carter still showed perplexity. But there was a hint of envy in his shrunken eyes. While he didn't understand all that Willis had in mind, he had enough confidence in the man's shrewdness to respect what he had said, although it was baffling to him. Then a furrow of doubt slowly showed on his forehead. "Well, supposing this miners' committee gets up a request for an assayer, too, then what?"

"Ben, I'm thinking ahead — just like I did on the sheriff's thing. I doubt if there's a miner among them that can think ahead. Anyway, even if they do, don't forget that we've struck first again. That's why I hurried back and drew up this petition. We strike first, see? Every time."

"I reckon," Carter said slowly. He was a little uneasy in the face of Willis's manipulations.

"Ben, Washington's always behind the times — slow as hell." Willis was watching the hawkish, thin features of the big man who stood before him. "If they act as slow this time as I reckon they will, I'll have it all and be gone before they wake up."

Willis's use of the first-person singular made doubts rise up again. "Will you need me?" Carter asked bluntly.

Willis shifted again in the chair. He had an

17

urge to laugh at Ben Carter for his dependence. "Of course, you'll fit in like always. We're a good team, Ben." He saw the renewed loyalty settle into Carter's eyes again and got out of his chair slowly, flexing his short, heavy legs. His feet had been bothering him lately; nothing serious, just an occasional sort of nagging ache.

He walked around the littered desk and stood where a shaft of early sunlight warmed his back. "Play the cards right, Ben, and it'll all come our way. I've already sent for the outside help we'll need. The whole thing ought to come off in a month; two months at the latest." The sun relaxed his shoulder muscles like an opiate.

Carter shuffled his feet, wondering at Willis's actions, his speed and perception with a little awe. The man struck fast when he moved — and surely. He should have known by then that with Harold Willis to approve was to act. He wagged his head in confusion. "Hell, Harold, I figured we was just talking. I didn't guess you'd already commenced the ball rolling."

Willis smiled out the window, not looking at Carter. He enjoyed seeing others bewildered by the swiftness of his actions. "Ben, I'm importing a man who'll raise a howl against me." He knew, without turning, that consternation was on Carter's face. There was considerable disaffection among the miners already for Harold Willis and his Gold River House. Willis was still smiling, an unpleasant, fixed smile. "This man'll agitate for everything we don't want; he'll get an assay office — that's the way I expect to fool this silly damned miners' committee. You see, Ben, if I got an office of my own, the miners wouldn't bring their gold in to me; this way, I'm starting opposition to myself so's the miners'll think I'm clear out of it."

Carter was beginning to understand. "Well —"

"Yeah," Willis said. "The miners'll go to the new man's office. He'll take the dust and flakes and stamp 'em into ingots or bars or whatever the miners want. The panners'll get back about two dollars worth of gold for every five dollars worth they bring in." Willis whirled, still smiling unpleasantly. "You see what I've got in mind now, Ben?"

Carter nodded. "Yeah, sure. But how do you know this hombre'll get the assay office?"

"Because he'll have more backing in the effort than the damned miners' committee'll have. He'll have part of the local support, plus all of my backing. Can't miss, Ben, it's that simple. Can't miss."

Carter was digesting the whole thing when

there was an abrupt knock at the door. Harold Willis called out for the visitor to enter. It was Neila. Ben's eyes tried to hide their sheen and only half succeeded.

Willis's wife went up close to the sheriff and smiled up into his face. "Ben, I've missed you." The sheriff felt the rusty blood mounting into his face, said nothing, but smiled. Neila reached up and ran her fingers under his chin. "Good looking devil, aren't you, Ben."

Willis's face showed minor irritation. It annoyed him the way Neila teased the lawman. His own glance swept over Neila with something like an ironic look in its depths. He nodded curtly at Carter. "All right, Sheriff, we both have things to do."

Carter smiled openly at Neila, who was watching him with an amused look, then turned toward Harold, nodded shortly, and walked out of the office.

The Gold River House was crowded with miners and drifters. There was a sprinkling of a new element, too; cowmen. Occasionally there was a freighter, shirt stiff with salt sweat; circulating, dusky women, leeching the men when and where they could, their harassed, hard faces wearing meaningless, stony smiles.

To Ben Carter it was always the same; in

a Kansas cowtown or an Oregon gold diggings. Violent, rough people of the frontier. He went on through the saloon, nodded to those who hailed him, and passed out on to the duck-boards beyond where the full fury of mid-day struck at the peeling, warped siding of Gold River.

The swiftness of Harold Willis and his brilliant duplicity were still in the forefront of Ben's mind, where he was grappling with them for understanding, when he went past the log café and glanced in at the low counter. He saw Cleve Simpson sitting there. A peal of laughter came out through the door to him and a snatch of a sentence, then he passed on.

"Cleve, you're the most solemn, serious man I've ever known."

Cleve's eyes held a faint twinkle moving in their depths. "Well, maybe. Cathy, how about us taking a livery rig and driving over to Ansell to the dance tonight?"

She still smiled, but the look was held over a little too long; its spontaneity was gone. "Sorry, Cleve." She said no more.

Cleve nodded, saying nothing for a second, then: "Well, some time else, maybe." Then his handsome head came up and the grey eyes looked squarely into her face and held there, drinking in the robust, abundant beauty of the

21

woman. "Any more of that blueberry pie, Cathy?"

"Coffee?"

He nodded and watched her disappear beyond the hanging curtain that separated her tiny kitchen from the counter. Cleve had always admired Cathy Brittan. She was a large, full-bodied woman with frank, level eyes and a wholesome look that even the lower element respected. She was probably the only woman in Gold River who could walk alone after dark through the town. She was a symbol to too many of the miners of what they had left behind in their search for wealth, and strangely enough they wanted her to stay that way. Gold River was many things and none of them very good, but its temper was swift, certain and murderous where Cathy was concerned. Many of the men had daughters her age, others had wives, too, and Cathy was the one thing they could look up to.

The food came and he ate. Cathy had a cup of coffee with him on a small stool behind the counter. He was almost finished and their desultory conversation was no more than an excuse to linger when Cathy said something that brought Cleve's head up, his glance staring fixedly at her.

"I understand you miners are going to buck Willis again and put up a town marshal."

"Who told you that?"

Cathy's blue eyes swung level to Cleve's face, saw the stillness of his stare, and she shrugged. "Some miner who was eating in here. I don't remember who it was exactly. Why, is it a secret?"

"Well, no," Cleve said. "But it's still just an idea. Willis ram-rodded Ben Carter over our man as sheriff. He beat us and we're still trying to get one man with authority on our side so that these night knifings and murders will stop." He let his eyes wander to the full richness of her mouth and faltered. "Aren't you interested in seeing Gold River amount to something, Cathy?"

She shrugged, looking past him out the door to where Ben Carter stood talking to the liveryman across the road. She liked the way Ben was put up. It was the knowledge of his reputation; the gun he carried under his coat plus the one on his hip; his friendship with Harold Willis — and other things, rarely spoken of and never proven, that made her leery of him. She took her glance away from the sheriff and looked down objectively at Cleve Simpson's handsome, sober face. She shrugged again.

"Cleve, these gold camps are all the same. They don't last. When the rich stuff is gone, the miners go, too." Her eyes went out the door again to the shacks and crudeness of Gold

River. "What is there to make this one any different from the others? Nothing. It'll die, too, won't it?"

Cleve smiled thinly. "Well, whether it lasts or not, Cathy, it doesn't mean that it must be lawless, too. No one knows how many men have had their throats slit in the night and had their purses stolen. Loose gold is an awful temptation." His mind slipped away wearily from the topic. "Cathy, what makes you stay in Gold River?"

"John Lenthall was my uncle, you know. I lived here with him before this was Gold River."

"But he's gone, Cathy, and that's what I mean; killings like his are unwarranted. Absolutely unnecessary — and you know that."

"Yes," she said dryly, "I know it, and you know it — and maybe others do, too, but that won't stop them, will it?"

"Of course not. Especially not if we all sit back and act passive, like a bunch of Siwash Indians. That's why we're getting up this committee. We — I want law in Gold River, so you can stay here, Cathy. That's what makes a town live on after the hi-grade is gone. We'll never have commerce without families."

She didn't know how to say it; she liked Cleve Simpson very much. She would like him even more if he wasn't so stuffy and solemn, so bent on diving head-first into the lion's mouth. Putting himself up as number one target for the villainous element headed by Willis's power. There was no way to tell a man like Cleve Simpson that he was endangering them all by his persistence in bucking organised crime. Cathy Brittan hated Willis as a symbol that stood for her uncle's murder, even though she knew he hadn't done the killing himself. Yet she didn't like the miners' way of fighting him, either. With little more than talk and threats and disorganised resentment, she knew that brutal retaliation would come down swiftly on their heads if they didn't stop. In actuality, she was a young woman in a rough atmosphere, and her need for security made her hate violence and fear it, too.

She shrugged again and smiled ruefully at Cleve. "I can't argue with you, Cleve. I know just what I feel, that's all."

Cleve got off the bench with a short nod and put some coins on the counter, looking thoughtfully at her. "We don't have to argue, Cathy, there's nothing to argue about. It's just the difference between right and wrong, that's all. Nothing to argue about, really."

"Is it worth getting killed over? For you, and the others who are with you, is it worth it?" She was admiring the strength in his face as she spoke.

He smiled at her. "There's not much difference in a man being dry-gulched for bucking Willis or having his throat slit in his sleep, is there? The choice — if there is one — seems to me to be better fighting the lawlessness in Gold River. Am I wrong?"

"No," Cathy shot back. "Not wrong, but surely likely to end in your death a lot faster."

Cleve shrugged. "That's something no one can answer. These night assassins can strike any time. Since Ben Carter's been sheriff, the killings have increased."

Nothing was said for a long moment between them. Cathy's coffee cup was empty and forgotten. They looked at one another across the counter, then Cleve leaned forward a little, looked intently into the blue eyes of the girl.

"Cathy, why don't you come to the meeting tonight? You'll see we're not as disorganised as you think. You'll also see that it's the miners themselves who want decent law in Gold River. There'll be merchants there, too. Listen to all of us before you decide we're firebrands and fools."

"Is there to be a meeting tonight, Cleve?"

"Yes, I reckon most of us will be there. Everybody should come. Everyone who wants Gold River to be something more than Willis's slaughter house, at any rate."

"Oh," Cathy said vaguely, pondering slowly, reluctantly. "It'll be all men, Cleve?"

He smiled. "Sure, that's it. Maybe next year it'll be womenfolk, too. But first someone's got to break the ice. It's not just me, Cathy — you'll see. It's all the boys who want to be able to sleep nights and not have to fear a bullet in the back when they're bent over their pans up the little creeks during the day."

She was mentally backing away. "Well, I don't think I ought —"

"Yes, you should, I'll guarantee you'll be treated as a lady. We need you, Cathy, we need every decent person in Gold River."

She looked at him, at the earnestness and appeal in his face, and laughed. The sound broke the spell of grimness that was settling in the little café. It was a soft, tinkling, musical sound. "Cleve, you're awfully serious about this, aren't you?"

His grey eyes crinkled slowly at their outer edges. "Sound like a preacher, don't I? Well, all right, call it anything you want, but we're going to have decent law and order in Gold River." He smiled a stubborn, fleeting grin with a self-conscious lacing to it and started for the door. "See you tonight."

Cathy Brittan still had the shadow of a whimsical smile on her face when the clump of Cleve Simpson's boots died out ahead of

27

the dull echo on the plankwalk. She cleaned up the counter listlessly. The weather had turned muggy again, like it did every afternoon, rain or shine. It sapped her energy. She washed the dishes in a shiny old pan she kept on the wood stove for that purpose, cleaned up the café, and went into her small, gloomy bedroom. There were no windows, glass was priceless in Oregon Territory.

She threw herself across the bed and relaxed. A picture of Cleve Simpson was fixed in her mind's eye. Her full underlip curled up in an unconscious little smile. He was so sincere in everything he did. So — well — intent and thorough. She drowsily thought of the curly black hair above the startling smoke-grey of his eyes, and the powerful chest and shoulders. He was a handsome man, but in another way so was Harold Willis's catspaw, Ben Carter.

CHAPTER TWO

The Miners' Committee

Cleve Simpson watched the end of a day in Gold River from the stingy porch overhang of his shack above the river. Miners, tired of the lasting drudgery of the river sluices, shuffled uptown toward the Gold River House. Several went toward Cathy's café.

As the sun went lower, the town gradually filled up. There were men afoot mostly, but here and there a rider bobbed along above the mob, and a less frequent wagon rumbled by. Everywhere, the Oregon dust and river mud clung like dried blood to the men and animals. There was a smattering of men who came down the river, bringing their flat-faced squaws or Chileños, poling or rowing stolidly in from lonely diggings farther inland, where the forests hid everything and the silence was like an eternity.

Cleve watched them congregate in the roadway and felt a deep satisfaction. This time, Willis wouldn't trick them at the last minute. Now his committee knew who they were fighting. It would be votes alone that counted, and Cleve smiled as he washed in the basin. The votes were jamming into Gold River by the hundreds — honest votes at that — and a majority as well.

It was close to nine o'clock before Cleve locked his cabin and walked into town. It was a warm, benevolent night, full of the fragrance of the river and the rank forests and the many pipes that sent their pungent aroma into the gloom.

Cleve drifted through the crowd, estimating their number; he was surprised, there were close to two hundred people, many of whom he had never seen before. Freighters and cow-men punching out little ranches inland and new miners, with a sprinkling of travellers and merchants and just plain strangers, uniden-tifiable with any of the endeavours of Gold River. He saw Cathy Brittan in a rent in the slow-moving, drifting, restless mob, and no-ticed she was wearing a shawl. Cleve smiled inwardly; it was just like her to wear a shawl for propriety, for the night was warm. Then he was grasped by the arm as he went close to the men congregated behind the crude stand that had been built for the speakers. He joined them, smiling at the determined, perspiring faces.

"Let's go!"

It was a cry that reflected the mood of the crowd. One of the committee men, a youngish, clear-eyed man named Sam Lamarr, gave Cleve a gentle shove. "Give 'em hell, hombre. Git on the box."

Cleve stepped up, looked down into the faces, and felt conspicuous in his clean white shirt. The babble died to a low hum. Cleve saw Cathy's shawl and her upturned face, and right behind her, standing close to Ben Carter, Neila Willis with her jet hair and black eyes, holding him in a fixed stare.

He spread out big hands and let them drop. The hum of voices died away until the soft chuckling of the river came to him from below the bluff of Gold River.

"Let 'em have it, boy!" shouted an old, grizzled, bent miner.

Cleve smiled briefly. "Folks, there's some of us that think Gold River's come of age. We figure we've got a sheriff now to take care of the outlying areas and now we want a town marshal to take care of Gold River itself. There's lawlessness here that'll keep any of us from bringing our families here; not just lawlessness, either. There's the problem of gold. All we got now is pokes; there's no way to get honest weight and States currency for our ore. You all remember the Miners' Bank coins, don't you?"

31

A derisive ripple of laughter ran through the crowd. They well remembered the great uproar when they learned that a spot check taken on the coins that had been minted on private capital proved to be worth less than half its face value. Again Cleve held his hands up for quiet.

"It's bad enough that we get shot in the back by day and our throats slit by night, but to get robbed as well on true weight, well — that's asking a miner to take too much. Gold River has no minted money; no law, no safety worth the name. For that reason, the miners' committee has called this meeting for tonight. Gold River needs a town marshal and an assay office. Until we get these things, there are a lot of us here tonight who'll be robbed and probably killed. I suggest we hold an election right away for town marshal and also support a miners' committee petition to the government for a branch mint here in Gold River. What do you say?"

The crowd thundered immediate approval. They had all heard the gist of what was to be said about a town marshal, and approved. Cleve and his committee had purposely kept from mentioning the assay office, hoping to keep Harold Willis in the dark until the last minute. They had no way of knowing that once more Willis was ahead of them.

32

When the tumult died down, Cleve had been unanimously elected by hand vote to head the miners' committee of Gold River. Sam Lamarr was the leader in this movement. He relinquished the stand again with a broad smile and waved Cleve back to the crowd.

Cleve nodded for silence, got it, and spoke again without smiling. "All right, boys, we'll go to work. I'd like to suggest that election day for the new marshal — or constable or whatever you want to call him — be next Wednesday. That'll give every candidate a week to campaign in. Above all, we've got to have law and order, and we want the same thing while we're trying to get it. Keep sober, boys, and cooperate. If you do this and back your committee one hundred per cent, we'll clean Gold River up like it should be."

Cleve stopped talking and listened to the shouts of the crowd. His face sought out Cathy; the shawl was conspicuous. The blue eyes stared up at him with a look of intensity. Cleve smiled ironically. Now she would see that there was more than one fanatic in Gold River.

Then his glance went to Neila Willis, beside Ben Carter. The sheriff's look was unpleasant, but, strangely, Harold Willis's wife was applauding along with the rest of the people. Cleve's smile twisted downward in a sardonic way; he guessed Neila to be far more clever and diplomatic than Ben Carter, whose antagonism was open and evident. But Cleve was wrong; Neila was smiling and applauding because she liked what Cleve had said, the way he had said it, and because *he* had said it.

The miners' committee adjourned to Cathy's café. The crowd dissipated gradually toward the stronghold of its enemy, Harold Willis, for the Gold River House was the only saloon, and as yet many didn't know or even suspect that Willis was the man who bought their stolen gold at discount from the night riders among them.

Ed Young, one of the committeemen, blew into his coffee, eyeing Cathy, who served them in silence with a blank face. "Listen, maybe we sprung this assay office business too soon; more'n we can chew, maybe."

Frank Pelham snorted: "Nope, I disagree. It's got to be done, like Cleve says, sooner or later, and we might as well get it rolling now. This way, we can get plenty of backing before Willis bucks us in it like he did in the election for sheriff."

Young said no more, but he didn't look convinced, either. Cleve sipped his coffee and looked at the others. "Don't stop, boys, keep arguing. Keep the ball rolling, that's how we'll make progress. Thresh out every problem as we come to it. Talk's cheap right now — and valuable, too."

"Yeah," said a small, wiry man who had been silent up until then. He was Perc Overholt, the clerk at T. Jones Emporium, who handled the banked dust for the miners who brought it to the massive safe because Gold River had no bank. Miners' shacks were proving very vulnerable to the nightly assaults by masked killers. "Cleve, I get to know things, running T. Jones's banking end of the store. The most surprising thing to old man Jones and me is the fact that Harold Willis came to us and traded us dust for minted money which he sent to the Oregon Bank at Jacksonville. He deposited ten thousand dollars over there to the account of a feller named Owen Byrd. Then Willis sent out a big shipment of dust to be used in posting bond."

The men were looking at Overholt closely. Sam Lamarr smoked and frowned, trying to guess what was behind Willis's move, then he shrugged in resignation. "Well, I give up; what's it look like to you, Perc?"

Overholt squinted. "Damned if I know. But just guessing, I'd say he's trying like the devil to get a government assayer sent in here. This Owen Byrd is the head assayer at Jacksonville. If Willis's money wasn't a bribe, why wasn't it sent directly to the branch mint instead of being deposited to Byrd's account? Like the dust, maybe!"

Cleve let the smoke trickle up his face. His grey eyes were bitter and ironic, and motionless, staring into and beyond Perc Overholt. He felt as if someone had just kicked him in the stomach. He had been clever in withholding information about the assay office, but, just like before, Willis had out-guessed him as smoothly, deftly and swiftly as he had in the election for sheriff. Anger welled up solidly in his chest. He controlled it with an effort, shot a glance at Cathy, saw her beautiful blue eyes on his face, and to his own astonishment, winked. The girl's eyes widened, colour climbed into her cheeks as Cleve looked hastily away.

"Harold Willis is smart; damned smart. Boys, if he's got Byrd, he's got the head man. You follow that through? If he's got Byrd, he can put his own men into the mint over at Jacksonville, and here, too — if we get a branch mint, because our mint'll probably be under the bigger office at Jacksonville."

Ed Young looked into his empty coffee mug. "That," he said with dawning shock, "means Harold Willis will control the assays on all the gold we pan and want minted, dammit!"

Sam Lamarr rubbed the outer edge of one ear before he spoke. "Y'know, if Willis owns

Byrd, there'll sure as hell be others. It won't be just Ben Carter and Byrd. In other words, for every one we know about, how many'll there be we don't have any idea about?"

A burly, bald man named Eric Schmidt struck the counter with a massive, scarred fist. "Listen, boys, this Willis is showing himself to be more'n the owner of the Gold River House. The more we dig, the more we uncover. I'll give you odds he's behind more'n just this sheriff deal and bribing the head assayer over in Jacksonville. Maybe he's even in on the killings — the robberies — that're going on here near every night."

Cleve raised his voice into the dour tumblings that threatened to break the meeting up into diverse tangents. "First off, let's decide on our own man for the town marshal's job."

Perc Overholt looked up. "Who's your choice, Cleve?"

"Sam Lamarr."

There was a thoughtful silence, then Schmidt's big fist came down again. "Me, too," he said. It became unanimous and noisy. Lamarr looked both confused and bewildered.

Cleve shot another barb into the bedlam. "All right, that's taken care of. Now, this assay office deal is a little different. Let's hear suggestions about it."

Ed Young looked up from manufacturing a cigarette. "Well, it seems to me we got to get a letter to the Territorial Legislature, asking for an assayer for Gold River, and another letter to Congress asking for a branch U.S. Mint for Gold River, too." Ed looked around questioningly.

Sam Lamarr nodded. "Yeah, I reckon that's the way, all right; but maybe we ought to write to Washington for a U.S. Marshal to be sent here until this thing's over with. My hunch is that all these robberies and killings aren't nothing to what we're going to have now that we're organised and getting set for trouble."

It was breaking dawn before the committee broke up its meeting. They had resolved their immediate problems into actions that took laborious stints of letter-writing before they settled back and mulled over their plans in general, found themselves unified in intentions if not always in accord. They closed their gathering with promises to consider Eric Schmidt's suggestion that they have a mayoralty election after the forthcoming election for a town marshal. Then Cathy, still wide awake and saying nothing but absorbing it all with kindled interest, went around to the wall brackets and blew down the lamp chimneys. Dawn had broken into a new day when the last of the committeemen, Cleve Simpson, filed out of her café.

Cleve turned, looked speculatively at the girl, and smiled. "Cathy, do you still think I'm courting disaster?"

She nodded up into his face. "More than ever now, Cleve, but —"

"Yes?"

"But I think you're right now. Not only right, but right enough to have good backing. Only, well, I'm afraid you'll be the main target, too, and that'll make you a marked man to every outlaw in the Gold River country. You'll have to be awfully careful, Cleve, awfully careful."

He looked at her for a minute without speaking, thinking how wonderful she looked after being up all night. Then he smiled, nodded, and went out into the weak light, where a slash of dawn had laid open the underbelly of the lowering darkness and disclosed the pinkness of a new day beneath.

Cleve had the door of his shack open and closed and had lit the lantern before he saw that he was not alone. His eyes widened in astonishment, for Neila Willis was sitting on the side of his bunk, smiling up into his face, and her black eyes were tantalisingly warm and uninhibited. Cleve didn't move.

Neila spoke evenly, still letting the boldness of her eyes hold his glance in a trap of surprise. "It's been quite a night, I take it."

Cleve's surprise turned to startled irritation. "What are you doing here, Missus Willis? How'd you get in?"

The woman's almost square shoulders rose and fell. "I got in easily; some day, if you're nice, I'll show you how it's done. No problem, though, with these miners' shacks."

"What do you want?"

"You!" She let the smile ripen, become possessive. "First, I wanted to congratulate you on your talk and on your success with the miners. You were good; very good. I like men who are sure of themselves." She got up slowly and crossed the room to Cleve and stood before him, not more than ten inches from him, still smiling and holding his glance with her own. "And, I want you. You — know what I mean?"

Cleve shook his head stubbornly. "No, I'm afraid I don't."

Neila laughed and took a swift step forward and sought for his mouth, pulling his head down with hands like talons that gouged painfully into his neck muscles.

Cleve reached up, grasped the firm, hard flesh of her arms and tore her away. His blood pounded like drums in his ears and the fever in him made an animal fury rage in his veins for this woman who was married to the man he was determined to pull down and destroy.

40

"You — you damned fool."

Neila's laughter came again, thick and harsh, then she cocked her handsome head to one side and looked up at him from beneath long, upcurving lashes. "By God, whatever else you are, Cleve Simpson, you're a man."

"What do you mean — whatever else I am?"

She shook her head. "Nothing."

"Why did you come here?"

She shrugged, coming close again. "There's something murderous in you, Cleve Simpson. I know it, if you don't; we're alike underneath, somehow, I think. That's why I came, to find out."

Cleve's amazement slowly turned to disgust and uneasiness. "Well, I don't know what you mean, but you'd better go."

"No, not yet."

"You fool, your husband'll be hunting for you if you don't get back."

Neila laughed again. "I don't think so. He's busy with a man who came in on the stage this evening, a Mr. Thorpe. You'd like to meet this Mr. Thorpe, I imagine, Cleve Simpson."

"Why?"

"For the hell of it; forget it." She came up to him again, the black eyes excited and challenging and cruel.

Cleve reached behind him, opened the cabin door swiftly and took Neila by the arm. "Get out," he said evenly, "and stay out — and tell your husband he'd better try some other way."

"No, my husband doesn't know anything about this. I give you my word."

"I don't believe you. Get out and stay out." He gave her a sharp shove, anger welling up thicker inside of him.

Neila swung back and raged at him, clawing with both hands. The taunts went into profanity and scorched him. He turned aside from the claws before his eyes and swung an open hand the size of a small ham. The jolt was controlled, but it sent Neila reeling, staggering back and fingering into the tight bodice of her dress.

Cleve moved swiftly, caught the wrist, and twisted savagely. She gasped, bit her lip, and the little gun lay in the dust. She didn't swear or cry. She just leaned there in the filth of the roadway and stared up at Cleve and licked at a little rivulet of blood at the corner of her mouth.

He scooped up the little gun, broke it, tossed the bullets away and flung the gun down before her. He shot an angry, aroused look at her and went into the shack, slamming the door.

When Cleve awoke, his mind was in a boiling tumult of conflict. He recalled what the members of the committee had said easily enough, and this brought up the extent of Willis's opposition and the scope of his domination. Through these thoughts ran the vision of Cathy Brittan, handsome and clear-eyed. He distinctly recalled the way she had listened to everything that had been said in her café the previous night and had absorbed it in silence.

Then another scene came into his mind and he shoved out of bed in shame and disgust. Neila Willis, her strange words and stranger violence, and, finally, the way she leaned over in the dirt of the roadway, staring up at him with that fixed, unearthly look in her coal black eyes. He swore under his breath and moved through the shack, feeling the nearness of sunrise.

In the thoughts that crowded his mind as he made breakfast were the girl's face and the woman's, side by side, mocking him. He fought clear of them and his mind fastened on the almost unbelievable things Perc Overholt had said at the meeting. Was it possible that Owen Byrd, known by all the miners as head assayer at Jacksonville, was actually bribed by Harold Willis, and, if so, was it because Willis didn't want an assay office in Gold River? Also, if Byrd was in Willis's employ, no matter where the assay office was actually located, there wouldn't be much chance of honest weight for the panners.

He sluiced out his breakfast utensils and dumped the oily water into the river and returned to his shack. He made a cigarette and sat on a bench along the wall, staring across the room.

Cleve knew that Harold Willis was the prime adversary to his committee. And Willis was wealthy and powerful — and merciless. Neila, too, was merciless, but in a different way. Cleve shook his head and scowled until he was back to the main subject. Remembering Neila's face angered him, but it dimly persisted in haunting his recollections of the night before. If Willis was fighting to control the assay office, then he wouldn't overlook the minting side of it, and Cleve knew this would be disastrous for the miners.

He mashed out his cigarette and slouched restlessly in the chair. Willis was their foremost enemy; Gold River would have to move fast and demand a branch mint, too. Once he had read of similar things in far places; when gold had been discovered in the Carolinas, the government had operated a branch mint at Charlotte. And back in the '30s, another branch mint had been operated at Dahlonega, Georgia, when gold had been found there. Cleve couldn't recall them specifically, but he knew that there had been other cases, too. Anyway, the thing crystallised into a slow conviction that Gold River must oppose sending their ore over to Jacksonville and must campaign for a branch mint and assay office in Gold River. Two pressure groups in the same area, petitioning for an assay office and branch mint, would make the importance of their needs evident back in Washington.

Cleve arose, stretched, and swore aloud to himself, summing it up: the war was on and every man in the camp must now take sides. The fight to divide and conquer, or to cooperate for victory, was in the balance.

He was turning away toward the door when someone knocked. He stared at the panel with uneasiness; the first thought that had come into his mind was that Neila Willis had come back. He was still standing there when the pounding became more insistent. He pulled the door open and used his body to block the passageway.

It was Cathy Brittan, her shawl carelessly around her shoulders, looking up at him in her big-eyed way, seeing the veiled truculence on his face. "Cleve, well — you look — rather formidable."

He blushed in confusion and stepped back. "I'm awfully sorry. It was just — nothing. Come in, Cathy."

The girl went past him and shot glances around the small, neat room, then turned back and faced him in the centre of the cabin.

"Cleve, I thought you ought to know this, it's — something important to you."

Cleve grinned at her solemnity so early in the morning. "What, Cathy?"

"Harold Willis has already petitioned for an assay office here in Gold River."

"The — devil." Cleve's grin died suddenly. The harassed look came back and his eyes dropped away from the freshness of her and looked at nothing. "Lord, that man's smart. If he beats us in this, we'll be beaten for good." He looked back suddenly. "How do you know this, Cathy?"

She coloured a little. "I heard Ben Carter telling a man named Thorpe — at least, that's what Ben called him — about it."

"In the café?"

"Yes."

Cleve made a wry face. "Carter's a fool, Willis would skin him alive for speaking out like that." He thought of Neila's words about a man named Thorpe. "Cathy, this man Ben was with — what was your impression of him? Did he seem to be a Willis man?"

She nodded. "Yes, indeed; he was a Willis man through and through. All you had to do was listen to them talk and you could tell that."

46

He nodded at her. "Well, thanks, Cathy." His eyes were on her face. "I thought you didn't want to get involved in this fight."

She shrugged. "I didn't; I still don't, either, but the whole camp seemed behind you last night at the meeting. I hate violence, Cleve, but — well, I reckon some of the enthusiasm rubbed off." She smiled at him. "Anyway, I know you're right. I know it deep inside, but it's the trouble that frightens me."

"Cathy, there isn't a worthwhile thing in life that wasn't had by somebody fighting for it, and someone else fighting to keep it." He shrugged slightly. "Running away from trouble won't work, either. I've seen it done before, but I'd like it a lot better if you'd just sort of stay neutral."

"Why?" Her face was frank and puzzled. "Yesterday you all but dragged me to that meeting."

"Yes; reckon there'll be real trouble now, and I don't want to see you in it, Cathy. Fighting with words is one thing; this'll be something else — no place for a woman." He winced. Neila's cruel face was smiling ecstatically at him from inside his head. He knew bitterly that she would love a brawl and revel in the agony of spilled blood.

"Cathy —"

"Yes."

"Why won't you ever go out with me?"

She didn't answer right away, and when she did her voice was gentle. "I've never gone out with the miners, Cleve. It's just — a policy of mine."

"I see; is it because they're miners — or just men?"

Again she hesitated. "I've seen them in town at night, Cleve." She didn't shudder, but he could sense the nearness of it under her shawl.

"Have you ever seen me with a Chileño?" It was blunt and gruff; he wanted it that way.

"No, Cleve, but — oh — I couldn't explain it to you in a million years. Please, let's not —"

"But, Cathy," Cleve said quietly, "I'm trying to tell you something I've wanted to tell you for a long time. I'm in love with you, Cathy. I don't want you like a Chileño. I want to marry you."

Cathy didn't move or speak. She was rooted to the floor, looking at him. There was none of the savage brilliance in his eyes she had seen on the faces of men before; there was something akin to dull anguish and a sincere, level look that seemed to typify Cleve Simpson to her. Without a word, she broke the spell and walked towards the door, white-faced and blinking.

Cleve didn't move until she was almost past him, then he reached out, caught her arm and turned her gently. "I'm sorry, I shouldn't have. It wasn't decent, was it?" He made a hopeless movement with his free hand. "I — didn't mean to take advantage of the way you came here to tell me about Willis." The hand dropped lifelessly to his side. "I'm sorry, Cathy."

The unexpected happened then; she moved close to him and stared up into his face for the space of a second, then her head was a blur and something warm, soft and moist brushed over his mouth and she whirled away and slammed the door of his shack behind her.

Cleve stood like a man in shock, afraid to move. The astonishment went out of him slowly and he fished for his tobacco pouch and the rumpled papers, fashioned a bulky cigarette without effort. He lit it and inhaled unconsciously, wondering thickly what motivated women, anyway. At first Cathy wouldn't become involved in Gold River's fight for order and decency; then she changed overnight and had taken the risk of warning him about the stranger, Thorpe. Then there had been a kind of mental inhibition about miners — about men in general — and then that had been swept away in an instant of rashness when she had kissed him and forever let down the barriers that had always seemed so unassailable to him. He smoked thoughtfully.

49

Could it be that women have automatic defences they used by instinct, only to discard them the same way — by instinct — when they sensed the uselessness — the meaninglessness — of them, when some inner judgment told them to do so? Cleve shrugged in perplexity and went out of the shack into the cool benevolence of early morning. The sounds of an aroused and stirring Gold River came abruptly and gratingly to him.

CHAPTER THREE

Willis and War!

Sam Lamarr entered Cleve Simpson's shack with a worried look. Eric Schmidt was close behind him. They sat without waiting for an invitation and Cleve took the sheaf of papers from Sam's hands, read them in silence, and looked up.

"Well, that settles that. I thought they were awfully sceptical about it last night. Not a one of them said a word all through the meeting at the café."

Sam nodded slowly, ponderously. "Yeah; well, we can do one of two things — elect four more committee members to take the place of the four who've just resigned, damn their yellow guts, or we can rut it with you, me, Perc Overholt and Eric here. That's what we came over about."

Cleve frowned. "It doesn't make much difference, Sam." He looked at the massive man beside Lamarr. "What do you think, Eric?"

"Four's enough; better we got four men ain't afraid 'n four hundred that are."

51

Cleve nodded. "That's good logic, Sam, and I'll go along with it. Have you talked to Perc? Maybe he'll want out, too."

"Yeah," Lamarr said. "We stopped at Jones's Emporium on the way over here; Perc don't look like much of a man, but you can't always tell. It's in the heart a lot of times — not just the muscle. Perc cussed these hombres out good and said he'd be buried some day, anyway, and would rather be a member of the committee when it happened than not."

Cleve smiled wryly. "I doubt if it'll come to that."

Sam Lamarr shrugged, saying nothing. In the silence the deep, rolling thunder of the stage vibrated through the shack.

Eric jerked his head sideways. "Stage's in, boys; let's go see what it brought."

They went out into the shimmering heat and watched the glistening horses stamping in the dust of their own backwash that drifted in and clung to them. It wasn't until the last of four passengers had gotten down and melted into the throng that always seemed to gather to watch arrivals that the three men exchanged glances.

One of the newcomers was a tall, lean, wolfish-looking man who wore two guns. He headed straight for the Gold River House. Trailing him was an older man, lean to the point of emaciation, sickly-looking and pale. They all recognised Owen Byrd, Head Assayer from Jacksonville. He, too, went toward the Gold River House.

Sam Lamarr turned and looked steadily at Cleve. "What you said back there in the shack — I wouldn't bet too much on it, Cleve. That first one was a gunman if I've ever seen one."

Cleve said nothing; he had read the signs, too, and fury uncoiled within him slowly. Willis was going to fight tooth and nail, that was evident now.

Eric touched Sam's arm lightly. "Come on, Sam, the election's only a few days off. We got to plug you to beat hell. If you don't win, boy, we're whipped. Then we'll have no law on our side."

But Sam did win — and easily, too — and there was a big rally in Gold River the night he was elected town marshal over some entries the miners had put up in half-hearted humour more than anything else. Cleve was uneasy about the victory. Willis had shown no interest in it, nor had he offered any opposition. Cleve was uneasy about a lot of things, and the way Cathy avoided him wasn't least among them — or the other thing that he refused to admit to himself existed: the secret way Neila Willis would come to his cabin at night and plead with him, argue and torment him. And last night she had screamed her fury at him and said he wouldn't be alive when the week was out.

The rally was Wednesday night — four more days before Willis's killer came after him. Cleve looked for Cathy in the crowd; he didn't want to die without telling her again that he loved her.

"Cleve."

"Howdy, Perc, what's got you all up in the air?"

Overholt shoved a thin newspaper into Cleve's hands and pointed with a rigid finger. "Look, read that. This here paper's from back east. My folks send it to me every once in a while. They sent me this one because of that column there. Some bird named Thorpe's petitioned for the assay office here in Gold River, along with us and Willis."

Cleve read by the flickering light of a small bonfire and the reason for Thorpe's presence in Gold River became crystal clear to him. He handed the paper back to Overholt with a crooked smile. "Damn! Willis is a genius."

"What?" Overholt said, pushing in close. "They're making so much noise that I can't hear. What'd you say?"

Cleve leaned toward the smaller man. "Willis is smart, Perc. Thorpe and Willis both petitioning makes odds two-to-one against us getting the assay office in Gold River the way we want it. Darn his soul, he's smart."

Overholt nodded, saying nothing and studying the paper in his hands as though it were a rattlesnake. Then he turned abruptly and stalked off through the crowd of miners, looking for Eric Schmidt and the new town marshal, Sam Lamarr.

Cleve saw Willis's man, Thorpe, talking to some miners. He watched from the shadows and saw the men laugh together. Making a wry face, he pushed through the swirl of people around the newcomer. When he was close, the miners greeted him and introduced him.

"Cleve, this is Lloyd Thorpe, an assayer who's thinking of opening an office here in Gold River."

Cleve's sardonic smile widened. "You're sort of looking Gold River over, is that it?"

Thorpe nodded benignly. "Yes, I used to be a government assayer in Georgia, Mr. Simpson. I'm at loose ends now, travelling through the gold fields looking for a likely spot to set up an office."

Cleve nodded. He baited the man easily. "The Lord knows that Gold River needs an assayer. When will you make the decision to stay here or go elsewhere, Mr. Thorpe? We need an assayer in the worst way. All of us would like to know you're going to stay."

Thorpe shrugged casually. "I'm not convinced there's sufficient business here to warrant applying for an assaying licence from the Territorial government, Mr. Simpson."

"No?" Cleve said coldly. "Then why did you apply for the permit a week ago, if you didn't know then — and still don't know — if you're going to stay in Gold River?"

The smiling miners looked from one man to another, sensed Cleve's hostility, and slowly understood what he was saying to the nattily-dressed stranger. Suspicion appeared like magic on their faces. They looked stonily at Thorpe. Waiting. Thorpe was too startled to speak.

Cleve went on, seeing the other man wasn't going to answer. "I'll tell you why you did it, Mr. Thorpe: because Harold Willis hired you for the job, hoping to split the miners against themselves — some backing you, some backing themselves, and maybe even a few backing Willis's petition. Yes, we know about that, too. It would make the chances of the miners themselves having an honest assay office and local mint just about impossible." Cleve leaned forward a little from his rugged height and lowered his voice. "Thorpe, you have exactly twenty-four hours to get out of Gold River!"

One of the listening miners detached himself from the group. The others drifted away after Lloyd Thorpe spun on his heel and became lost in the crowd.

Cleve was still standing on the fringe of the gathering when Cathy came up and touched his arm. He turned slowly, looking at her with troubled eyes. The girl's face was drawn and tense. "Cleve, I'm happy for you. This is a definite victory over Willis."

He relaxed and smiled wryly. "Well, yes, but as fast as the miners win one round, Willis already has another one in motion." He levered up a smile, looking at the virile beauty of the girl. "Cathy, why have you been avoiding me?"

She reddened a little. Her eyes fell, too. "That's not a fair question, Cleve."

"Why?" he asked, puzzled.

"Because — I want to be sure, Cleve. Really certain. It takes time with a woman."

He nodded, thinking of Neila's fury when she had told him he wouldn't live out the week. "I hope it doesn't take too long, Cathy."

There was something grim in his voice that made her look up swiftly. "Why do you say that?"

"I want to marry you. I want to tell you how much I love you; and show you, Cathy. That's all. We could ride over to Ansell or

Jacksonville and be married tonight or tomorrow."

She didn't answer. Her blue eyes went over his face slowly, dreamily. "I'll give you your answer tomorrow, Cleve; is that all right?"

He smiled softly. "It'll have to be, I reckon. When you're thinking about it, Cathy, remember that I love you more than — than —" he thought ironically before he said, "life."

Cathy watched him stalk toward the little knot of men around the smudge fire. Her eyes were troubled, but there was something infinitely greater than any trouble moving back in their depths, too; love for this solemn man she had thought stuffy, once, and now knew instead as an uncompromising idealist. She turned, saw Neila Willis standing in the shadows looking at her without moving, shuddered in spite of herself, and went toward her café.

Sam Lamarr was wagging his head good-naturedly at Eric Schmidt. "Hell, Eric, we don't have anything for *one* lawman to do tonight, let alone deputy marshals."

"No," Eric persisted gruffly, "not yet. But dammit all, Sam, you know how the diggings are being torn up by these night riders. Listen, all I'm saying is that if you'd deputise three or four of the boys, you could have fear of the law in every renegade among us in twenty-four hours."

Cleve interrupted with no effort. The other men had seen him coming and stood waiting. "He'll need deputies, Eric, but let's not do it all tonight. Let's wait until tomorrow and do it right and carefully. We've got to meet tomorrow, anyway. There's this business of setting up an election for a mayor, too."

Eric squinted at Cleve. "All right. What's this talk that's going around about this stranger, Thorpe?"

Cleve told them about Overholt's newspaper. They listened in amazement, then reacted differently. Eric swore sulphurously and briefly, glared at the thinning crowd, then shrugged fatalistically, saying nothing, and looked back at Cleve, waiting.

Sam Lamarr scratched his nose and screwed his face up. "Cleve, let's meet at your diggings after breakfast; all right?"

"Yeah." Cleve turned to Eric. "Will you pass the word to Perc?" The heavily-muscled miner nodded stolidly, still angry, and the men moved away.

Cleve went towards his shack with a heavy heart. He couldn't shake off his feeling of depression, although he had less reason now for feeling that way than before the election.

He entered his shack and smelt cigar smoke.

59

The stranger was taller than Cleve, but thinner. His face was pale and puffy and possessed of soulless, faded blue eyes that looked out on a world through a maze of warped emotions. He nodded brusquely, got off the bench and watched Cleve close the door and appraise the two guns hanging at the narrow hips.

"What do you want here, mister?"

The answer came back swiftly enough. "Cleve Simpson?"

"From Willis, I reckon; I saw you get off the stage today."

The cigar went back into the man's thin, bloodless slash of a mouth, and the wide eyes whipped over Cleve's frame in a darting appraisal. One hand always hung within inches of a gun-butt. "Yeah, from Willis. But that's not all of it; I got a proposition for you."

Cleve had a Derringer in his trousers pocket, but he wasn't fool enough to try for it. He nodded. "I'm listening."

The gunman spoke in a husky voice. "You've guessed who hired me. All right, no sense in going over that."

"No," Cleve said, wondering.

"I'm supposed to kill you; I'll probably do it, too. But in cases like this, where I personally don't give a damn either way, the job boils down to a question of money. Willis promised to pay me five hundred dollars when

I toss your wallet on his desk. How much'll you pay not to have it taken off your corpse?"

Cleve reached up and slowly scratched his ribs. He felt nothing — neither like nor dislike — for the killer, even though the man was making him a price on his life. He shrugged. "Hell, I don't have much money. You'd have to have it all right now?"

The gunman nodded, still smoking and watching Cleve with two dead eyes. There was a sort of grim, bitter humour in the situation; Cleve almost smiled to think that Willis's killer would sell him out. He allowed a trace of a grin to form at the corners of his mouth when he thought of the look of incredulity he would see on Willis's face when the fat man would see Cleve the next morning — very much alive.

"You're going to ride out of Gold River as soon as you see Willis?"

Another nod. "Yeah; either way, I won't be here half an hour after I walk out of this shack."

Cleve nodded. "All right. I've got four hundred in States currency — paper — and I'll give you another four hundred in dust. That suit you?"

The gunman nodded. There was an interested gleam in his eyes now; almost a pleasant look. "That's fine; get it."

Cleve studied the man closely. There was the chance of a double-cross. He shook his head. "Not so fast. What proof have I that you won't blast me as soon as I hand you the money?"

"None," the gunman said. "None at all; just that I don't work that way."

Cleve smiled openly. "I reckon I've got to take the chance, but I don't mind telling you that I figure a man that'll sell out one boss, would sell out another." The gunman didn't answer, just shrugged. Cleve had an idea that appealed strongly to him. "Listen, I'll go you one better; don't get this movement wrong." He fished out his wallet and held it out after removing the money. "Take this back to Willis and collect his bounty, too."

The gunman's face was impassive. For a second, he made no move to accept the wallet; then he reached out with his left hand and took it, still holding Cleve with his eyes. There was a strange, odd glint of humour on his pale face, then he rocked his head back a little and laughed. "By God," he said, laughing again, "that's a good one. I'll be damned if it ain't. That's the best one I've ever run across. You figure to make this Willis lose his wad, too, if you have to lose yours. You're clever — darned if you ain't. By God, I like that."

He studied Cleve for a long moment, then

looked at the bundle of carefully-hoarded paper currency in his hand. He realised that paper money was a rarity in Oregon Territory. He nodded towards it. "You got four hundred there?" Cleve nodded. "All right," the hired gunman said, "that's enough; I'm human, too. I like a laugh. Keep the dust and give me that paper money. You've earned the dust. I'll get Willis's five hundred. That'll make close to a thousand dollars for not killing a man that I'd of got five hundred for killing."

Cleve handed over the money and watched the renegade stuff it uncounted into a grimy trousers pocket.

The gunman was looking at him blankly again. "Listen, Simpson; for the dust, you've got to stay in this shack for an hour. I'll need that time to get clear of Gold River with Willis's money. All right?"

"Don't worry; you're safe as far as I'm concerned. I'll get my money back."

"From Willis?" the gunman asked speculatively, looking at the powerful build of his intended victim.

"Yeah, from Willis — with interest, too."

The gunman walked slowly forward, jerking his head for Cleve to stand clear of the door. "I reckon you will at that," he said dryly. "Don't fault me, Simpson; just stay out of sight for an hour. After that, Willis is yours."

63

Cleve stayed in his cabin the rest of the night. It wasn't until an hour before sunup that he arose on one elbow, and watched a knife blade scratching between the door and the jamb, feel tentatively for the bar, come up under it and raise the bar enough for the door to be opened. Cleve came noiselessly out of the bedding, held the Derringer in his hand, and waited on the far side of the panel as it slowly swung inward.

He saw the oval beauty of Neila Willis's face as she came into the cabin, looking at the floor with a twisted, anticipatory smile holding the heavy, rich contours of her mouth up at the corners. Then he cocked the little gun, and the noise made her spin, face twisted in horror when she saw him in the pale, watery light, glaring at her with death in his eyes.

"Cleve! Oh, Cleve, darling!" It had a fervent lilt to it, but there was a tincture of disappointment that rode with the words into the stillness.

"Sorry to disappoint you, Neila; you and your husband."

"How — did you do it?"

"It wasn't hard. Drop the knife, Neila." She did, opening her hand without looking away from his face. "Over here, by the bed, and stand still."

She backed away, the first shock gone and

the jet-black eyes piercing the gloom and tracing the outline of his body in the shadows. There was a new fire writhing in her eyes when he came over, reached up and spun her away. He quickly felt for a gun, found none, and stepped back, dropping the Derringer back into his trousers pocket on a bench.

He faced her with less than a foot between them. "Why did you come back? Did you expect to see a corpse, Neila?"

"Cleve; it was something — that made me come back. I had to."

"Disappointed, too — aren't you?"

"Cleve — I'm not; no." She went up against him as she had before, her lips seeking his in the darkness.

Cleve felt the pressure of her mouth. For a second he imagined the gentle, shy touch of Cathy's kiss, and let his own mouth respond.

His muscles bulged under the tawny resistance he met, but he managed to push her away from him. He was standing there, looking at her — when there was a sharp gasp at the door. Cleve spun in time to see the dread and illness on Cathy's pale face, then the girl had turned away and the sound of her racing footsteps down the deserted plankwalk echoed like a knell in his ears.

It was Neila's laughter that brought him

back. She was standing there, raging in the dying ashes of her savage passion with uneven, spasmodic breathing, and she was looking down at him where he sat dully, stupidly, on the wall bench, and laughing at him.

"Your shack gets its share of dawn visitors, Cleve; by Criz', there's one that won't be back." Her laughter was musical and thrilling. He fought against it as he rose and went towards her. Neila's eyes blanked over in fear, then she whirled and ran out of the doorway.

Cleve was still alone when Sam Lamarr brought the news. He had got it from Perc Overholt at Jones Emporium, where the mail had been distributed. The whole story was contained in a cryptic passage in an Oregon City newspaper. Cleve took it, held it out and read it, forgetting Sam and Neila — and Cathy. The bile seeped into him as he read, and it sickened him. Each line was like a hammer-blow of defeat aimed at humbling him, personally.

"Congress in the States has finally authorised the following concerns to operate licensed assay offices, and stamp bars, ingots and/or coins in denominations not to exceed actual gold content, for Territorial and States usage in the gold field areas of the Far West: —

Norris, Grieg & Norris, Benecia City, California.

*The Massachusetts & California Company,
California.*

Templeton Reid, San Francisco, California.

HAROLD WILLIS, JACKSONVILLE, OREGON
TERRITORY.

Pacific Company, California.

Moffat & Company, California."

Cleve handed the paper back to Sam and
followed up with a sober glance at the town
marshal. "Well, Sam, he's taken us again."

Lamarr was alarmed at the dull tonelessness
of Cleve's voice. He began to make a cigarette,
and frowned at the thing in his hands. "Cleve,
it's not hopeless. Listen — Eric, Perc and I
have been up since before dawn." Cleve's eyes
swung quickly to the marshal, but Sam didn't
see the look. "We've been campaigning." He
lit the cigarette and looked up swiftly. "By
unanimous approval of all the men we've seen,
Cleve Simpson is the miners' choice for mayor
of Gold River."

Cleve's astonishment was real. Sam sliced
the air rapidly with a hand. "Now wait a second, Cleve; please — don't refuse, pardner.
The boys're hit hard by this victory of Willis's;
they're pretty darned beat right now. If you
let us down, we might as well all pack and
drift and let Willis have the river and the gold,
too. We're near the breaking point; there's
just one thing — one man — that'll hold us

67

together: you, as mayor."

Cleve listened; his shame became a background for the challenge that was before him. It would mean more than sniping if he accepted — and he had to accept. Harold Willis would see that he was killed as soon as his candidacy was announced. He knew it. He knew, too, that his own popularity was all that could finally turn the scales, and that his life wouldn't be worth a pan of sand if he did accept. Still, the decision wasn't hard. He nodded to Sam Lamarr, the bitterness in his eyes misinterpreted by the other man.

"All right, Sam; but let's have an election as soon as possible. We can't let Willis beat us on this, either — or we're finished completely, you know."

Sam smiled his relief and wagged his head. "He won't. Eric's got the boys circulating today. There won't be any gold panned until day after tomorrow. The election's to be tomorrow."

Cleve blinked, and slowly a cold smile spread out over the ruggedness of his face. "Darn you, Sam, you're the best of the lot."

Harold Willis took the incredible news of Simpson's candidacy, and the sudden decision to hold the election one day later, with a stunned look. For once, he hadn't anticipated the miners' canniness, and was caught wide of his goal.

Fury made Willis cold and silent. He sent for Ben Carter, and was closeted with the sheriff for three hours. Neila could hear their voices rise occasionally in heated argument, then drone along in staccato bursts of harmony. She watched Ben Carter leave her husband's office, and followed him out on to the duckboards, hesitating, letting her eyes do what she didn't dare to do — go with Ben down the road towards the livery-barn, where he disappeared inside. She saw Sam Lamarr, and three of the men he had deputised, heading briskly towards Cleve Simpson's shack, and her eyes kindled strangely.

Cleve was coming up from a bath in the river when Sam came to the shack, saw him and waited. "What's up, Sam?" The woodsmoke grey eyes went sardonically over the deputies. "You got your whole army with you."

Lamarr was uneasy and sweaty-faced. He was a boyish man with an infectious grin and a great sincerity. "Dammit, Cleve, we've been talking this over; Willis is mad as hell, and he's made threats we've all heard. We — all of us —" he waved at his deputies, "decided that we've got to lock you up overnight for your own safety. Willis has offered five hundred for you dead, boy." Lamarr's grin was undecided and nervous. "Please, Cleve; I know what you're thinking of this idea, but we've got to get you elected."

"Kind of like running away, isn't it, Sam?" Cleve asked mildly.

Sam shook his head vigorously. "I knew you'd figure that way, Cleve. Dammit all, it isn't; Willis'll get you killed. That'll just about finish the committee and all of our plans, too. See it that way won't you?"

Cleve nodded dourly. "All right, Sam."

They went uptown — Sam Lamarr and Cleve — with the three armed deputies flanking them. Just before they turned into the gaol, Cleve saw a large barge being poled up the river. He looked at the men, recognised none of them, shrugged and guessed them to be newcomers, then he went inside and took the .44 pistol that Sam handed him. Cleve also took a battered Hawkin rifle with a bag of loads, then settled into the small iron cage that was Gold River's gaol, just behind the marshal's desk in the shack the miners had erected for Lamarr.

The marshal sent for Eric Schmidt and Perc Overholt. He was nervous, and he showed it. Eric was sent to round up guards, while Overholt took over patrolling the town with four hard-bitten members of the miners' committee supporters. Eric's men guarded the gaol-house outside, while Sam and two others remained inside, armed to the teeth, prepared to resist any attempted assassination of the mayoralty candidate.

It was five minutes short of two o'clock in the morning when one of the deputies on guard outside the gaol called in to Lamarr: "There's some kind of racket up the road, Sam."

The marshal and one of his deputies peeped out of the doorway. By then, it was obvious what was happening: a dray wagon with the tongue lashed high in the air and the wheels set in place, loaded with small, burly casks, was gathering momentum as it was given a final heave down the road towards the gaol-house.

Sam's mouth was working. He could see the pitch sapling tied under the wagon, with the end flaming in a gorge of black, oily smoke, below the casks. The drops of pitch burned brightly in the manure-stained roadway to mark the progress of the lethal cargo.

Lamarr spun to his deputy. "Get Cleve out of the cell. Stay with him. Take him any place, but move fast. Lay low until you can get word to us telling us where you are. Beat it!"

The deputy needed no urging. His face reflected the flickering light on the oncoming wagon. He hurtled himself away at top speed.

Sam Lamarr knelt and deliberately began firing into the powder kegs, hoping to shatter them enough to hasten the explosion before the rocketing vehicle crashed into the shack that was his office.

A man dashed away, running with eyes starting out in abject horror. Sam saw him go by and watched another man loping stiffly towards him, crying out a warning. He recognised Perc Overholt, then turned back to firing into the rapidly-advancing wagon.

Cleve heard the bedlam and raced outside with Sam's deputy at his side. The Hawkin rifle dangled from one fist and his pistol was cocked in the other. He saw it all in a split second and raced away, ducking low, the picture of the great vehicle rolling over Sam Lamarr as fresh as daylight in his mind. Then the explosion ripped the night into a thousand violent echoes that chased one another in a tremendously crushing roar over the vast distances in every direction.

Gradually, silence came back, more awful than the explosion itself, and settled over Gold River along with the dust and debris that fell back in a diminishing racket of small noises until the town was like a tomb.

Men came running from every direction. Flames were licking into the other buildings, and miners in night-dress, others wearing little else beside boots and trousers, made hastily-formed bucket brigades that stretched like a writhing snake from the river. Gold River, from where Cleve leaned against a tree on the outskirts of the town and looked back, was a gaunt silhouette of dark against the hundreds of small fires that were born of the firebrands that fell from the skies like a scourge from the night. Cleve felt weak in the stomach and a listlessness swept over him. He turned, saw the deputy sitting shocked and speechless in wide-eyed terror beside him, then he turned back.

The battle raged in smoke, and dust that flew over the town on draughts created by the uneven battle added to the hellish spectacle. Like wraiths, men ran and shouted and battled with mad zeal to hold their own. One thing saved Gold River from complete destruction, even more than the efforts of the fire-fighters: a summer thunderstorm had turned the earth to soup and made the lichen freshen on the north sides of trees a few days before. The humidity and soddenness of the blotter-like siding and planking gave enough resistance to the flames to allow the sweating, panting bucket brigades to gain, slowly but inexorably, over the stubborn flames.

Before dawn, Gold River was smouldering

in a sullen pall of charcoal gloom, damaged and badly bedraggled, but still alive and standing.

Perc Overholt accepted a mug of coffee from Cathy and grunted a hoarse thanks. "Perc, wasn't Cleve — in there?" He saw the tragedy in her blue eyes, and nodded without speaking. The girl went on, lugging her big pot with its steaming liquid, and held out the tin cup, refilled, to the next man. Perc watched her go and made a cigarette, looking thoughtfully after her until Eric Schmidt came up. Then Perc faced the larger man, saw the scorched, blistered face and bare eyebrows.

"Eric, have you seen Sam or Cleve?"

The miner shook his big head. There was an irrational light in his eyes. "No; the last anyone knows, they were in the gaolhouse. They're gone, Perc; Willis has licked us. All right, let's take guns and go up there and kill him."

"Lynch him," Perc said quietly. "I'd like to, Eric. By gawd, I'd like nothing better on earth. We can't do it, though."

"Why not?" Eric asked simply.

"Because, dammit, that's exactly what we're fighting against. Cleve and Sam'd both bear me out, Eric; we're fighting mob violence and lynch-law and gun-law."

"G'almighty," Eric roared, so that the men passing by, bleary-eyed and shuffling with exhaustion, turned sunken, swollen eyes on him. "We're fighting fire with fire, Perc."

Overholt didn't look at the large man at all. He stood there shaking his head, matted with filth and seamed with old sweat. "All right," Eric said after a long moment. "All right, Perc; we won't. We won't do a thing until we've looked into this. We'll make a regular goddamned investigation, like Sam and Cleve'd do." His eyes flamed craftily again. "Then, when we got all we need, we'll hang the son of a — from the old oak in front of the livery-barn. We'll hang him so high, folks'll be able to see him for a hunnert miles!" Eric spun abruptly and stalked off with his head high and challenging. He passed Ben Carter, where the sheriff was standing back in the shadows, hesitated, saw Ben stiffen, and lashed out with an arm like an oak log that felled Carter where he stood, one hand half-drawing his gun, senseless in the dirt. Eric surveyed the sheriff in raw fury, stepped back and swung a murderous kick into the unconscious man's ribs, and walked away without looking back.

The wild night gave over, and order after a fashion had been restored by eight o'clock. Order and a smouldering, seething fury that was flaming in the miners as the indications pointed up the cause — and probable source — of the wheeled juggernaut that had turned Gold River into a shambles.

One of Sam Lamarr's guns was found fifty yards from the hole in the ground where the gaolhouse had stood. It was twisted almost beyond recognition. His left boot was unearthed behind the rubble of what had been his office. They never found Sam; just the one shattered gun and the boot.

Election day was a silent time of pathos. Sam's gun and boot were buried, with a long procession of dry-eyed miners watching.

There was little drinking, although the men were groggy on their feet and sick from burns and exhaustion. They held their election with a formidable bitterness, and Ben Carter, his broken ribs held together by generous bandaging, watched from the reasonable security of the Gold River House.

The fire was out, the marshal was buried, and no sign of Cleve Simpson was found, although the election had been carried out by the insistence of Eric Schmidt and Perc Overholt. The miners were standing around, lost, confused, leaderless and thirsting for blood, awaiting only the leadership that would guide them against everything Harold Willis stood for.

Then the cry went down the road that Cleve Simpson was coming into Gold River from the south end of town. Men didn't believe it, but ran out with the others, looking. The cries and shouts became roars that drew all Gold River out on to the plankwalk.

Cleve came down the middle of the road, still gripping the pistol that Sam had pressed into his hand, cocked and held lazily, easily, at his side. He didn't return the shouts. The deputy was behind him, narrow-eyed and watching the gathering throng. He, too, carried a cocked pistol in his hand.

Cleve went up to the wreckage of the gaolhouse, stared at the hole where Sam Lamarr had fought at the cost of his own life, and finally went over to a bench to sink down as nearly whipped as he had ever been in his life.

The polls in Jones Emporium closed before noon. Eric Schmidt had charge of the men who counted the votes, and it took slightly over an hour for the beaming Eric to determine that Cleve Simpson had won by a landslide vote, write-ins getting less than thirty-one votes in all.

Eric brought the news to Cleve where he sat with Perc Overholt and a large throng of silent, watchful men, all armed and waiting for something that they didn't know themselves.

Cleve thanked Eric and looked around. His eyes settled finally on Overholt. "Perc, Sam's got to have a successor; it's got to be in order, though." He looked at the men around him; one of them, a tall, muscular, blond teamster, was smiling. Cleve nodded towards him. "You're the first, pardner."

The blond man looked puzzled. "First what, Cleve?"

"First alderman." Others were appointed swiftly. Under Cleve's guidance, they passed the resolution appointing Perc Overholt temporary town marshal.

"Perc Overholt," Cleve said, "step up here."

"Yes, Cleve — ah — Mr. Mayor."

"Raise your right hand." Cleve swore Perc in as town marshal until another election could be held, then he nodded grimly towards Perc. "Your first job, Marshal, is to find out who started that wagon towards the gaolhouse, apprehend him and bring him before the miners' committee for trial." He waved his free hand towards the ravished town. "We want the man who did this, Marshal."

Perc Overholt turned away, searching the crowd for Lamarr's deputies. He took them and headed a straight line for the Gold River House. There was a taut silence while he was inside, then the men relaxed, for the marshal emerged with a puzzled, worried look and hurried to Cleve.

"He ain't in Gold River, Cleve; now what?"

"Is his wife here? Ben Carter?"

"None of 'em. The barkeep says they all left yesterday afternoon."

A voice in the crowd yelled out indignantly: "That's a damned lie. Ben Carter was here this morning. I seen him in the Gold River House, my own self."

Cleve nodded gently. "Carter can wait. We don't want Willis to get away. My guess is that he went to Jacksonville."

"Then we'll ride!" Overholt spat out.

Cleve got up, holstered his handgun and frowned. "All right, Perc; you'll ride with me. We'll take two of your deputies, but no more. We want Willis alive, not hanging from a tree."

Eric Schmidt swore angrily. "Cleve, we've all got a stake in this."

Cleve nodded. "Sure, Eric, I know. But I also know what would happen if we all went over there. We'd have a regular war. Gold River doesn't want that. Do me a favour, Eric; stay here and watch the town — see if Ben Carter's still here, too. Sort of get things back in order. You can do more'n Perc and me together."

Schmidt was looking into Cleve's face. The

wan, ill look shocked him. He nodded slowly, feeling pangs of pity for Cleve Simpson. "All right; just bring him back, boys. That's all I ask — just bring the murdering buzzard back!"

Cleve looked at his friends with a wry shake of his head. "Boys, we've got to rest a while. Going up against whatever's over in Jacksonville, done in like we are, isn't going to help our cause or our gun arms. Let's get some rest somewhere."

The ride to Jacksonville was made during the murderous blast of full summer heat. Arriving in the village, the four men threw themselves down in the shade of the local livery-barn and slept. Cleve was tired to the bone; before he could drift off, though, he thought of Cathy, and a poignant sadness held him. His mind was still sunken in the purple pathlessness of his quandary when sleep finally overcame him.

While Cleve Simpson, Perc Overholt and the two deputy town marshals slept like the dead, Harold Willis and Owen Byrd sat in the Gold River hostelry owner's room in the Turlock Hotel and tightened their strategy. Willis advanced Byrd additional funds for the immediate completion of the enlarged and newer assay office; Byrd, as anxious as the saloon man to mulct the panners, had already put a construction gang to work. Willis, however, did not tell the federal man of the violence he had engineered in Gold River; Byrd was not a young man, nor a daring one. Being in any way connected with a murder would obviously horrify him. Willis was no fool when it came to reading men, either. He allowed his confederate to know exactly what he wanted him to know, and nothing more.

The day was well spent when Cleve roused his companions. Watery-eyed and thick-tongued, they trooped to the public watering trough and dashed the last of their sleep away, washed after a fashion, combed their hair and felt considerably fresher than they had at any time in the past twenty-four hours.

"You got a plan, Cleve?"

"Just one. Hunt Willis and Carter and take them back with us."

Fred, a red-faced, freckled deputy, grunted. "I don't reckon we dare ask Jacksonville law for a hand — do we?"

Cleve shrugged. "Well, it'd probably be better, but it might complicate things."

The other deputy wagged his head solemnly. "To hell with 'em. We don't need 'em, anyway. Just find our man, stick a gun in his guts. . . . That's all we got to do. He'll come along all right."

"And if he don't?" Fred shot back.

"Pull the trigger!" came the short answer.

Perc darted a wry smile at Cleve. "Hope it don't come to that. Gold River's got its heart set on seeing Willis alive — long enough for a miners' court to try him, anyway."

Cleve had been studying the little town. There was an air of age and languor beneath the huge trees. Urchins played barefooted in the road; top buggies, a rare sight in Gold River, were common here. Jacksonville was old, established, staid and lasting. A man could sense it. Even after the gold fever had left, Jacksonville would linger.

Up the roadway, a working crew of men were making ready to erect a new building. There was an interested crowd of watchers, out for their late afternoon stroll, lingering in quiet curiosity around the roped-off lot.

Cleve eyed the crowd speculatively and nodded towards it. "Let's see who's in the crowd. That'll be a starter. If the folks we want aren't there, we'll commence hunting through the hotels and bars."

But Cleve wasn't wrong; they went into the crowd and mingled, four heavily-armed men whose clothing was thick with road dust and dried sweat, unshaven, dirty and hard-looking, cold-eyed and determined.

Cleve felt the fingers dig down into the flesh

of his arm and stay, gouging, straining with all the strength in the arm that guided them; he turned. Neila's eyes, shining black and pinpointing him above a small, bold smile, were startling.

"You didn't disappoint me, Cleve." She said it so calmly, so confidently, that he was shocked. "I knew you were too smart to die." The late sun was dancing in the blue-black of her hair when she shook her head. "I told Harold so."

"He didn't believe you?" Cleve asked sarcastically.

"No, of course not. Harold's infallible — to Harold."

Firmly, Cleve took her wrist and forced the hand away. "Where is your husband, Neila?"

She smiled wider. "You'll never find him, Cleve — never in God's green world. Unless — I tell you." She looked away, nodding towards the sweating labourers. "See this? It's the new assay office. Harold advanced the money to start construction. The assayer'll pay him back when the government funds get here."

Cleve's eyes widened. Harold Willis moved fast. He faced back to the handsome woman. "Byrd's your husband's man, isn't he?" At Neila's smile and silent shrug, he made a soft, unpleasant sound that resembled a laugh. "It's common knowledge, Neila. At least with the miners' committee."

Neila looked suddenly among the crowd; the twist of her little grin became sardonic. "You didn't come alone, I see. Well — go to it; you won't find Harold unless. . . ."

"Unless?"

"Unless — I want you to."

Cleve was studying the beautiful, evil face, saying nothing. Neila was assured, he could see that. He nodded brusquely, grimly.

"All right; then I think you'd better want to."

"Do you?" she challenged dryly. "Come along, follow me and don't bother looking for your friends. Two of them have already struck out across the road. They'll look through the hotels and saloons. Well, maybe *you'll* find my husband — but *they* won't!"

The woman threaded her way out of the little crowd of watchers. Cleve had little choice; he followed. When they were apart from the mob, close to a small iron bench beneath a huge and ancient cottonwood tree, Neila sat down and motioned to Cleve. Dourly he sat beside her, waiting. There was a small scowl above his eyes. She turned, saw the look and laughed at him.

"Harold's still my husband, Cleve. You know that. There's no love between us, I sup-

84

pose — certainly not on my side — but still, I owe him some loyalty."

"Loyalty aside," he said growlingly, "he's also responsible for more trouble than you can shake a stick at. Destruction, murder, theft, to name a few of the things we want him for."

"You didn't bring your men from Gold River, drive yourself like a slave — to tell me these things." She laughed again, teasing him. "You wouldn't want my help, anyway — with the conditions I'd put on it — or would you?"

He didn't answer; just let his lip curl a little, reflecting the contempt and scorn in his eyes.

Neila leaned forward, the smile gone now, an intense, feline expression on her face. "You're lucky, Cleve Simpson — damn you! Luckier than you know. Jacksonville and Gold River both have hordes of men who'd knock you down and trample over you to follow me. Not just Harold, either."

Cleve was startled by the impassioned seriousness in her eyes. There was a strangely beautiful cruelty that fitted, oddly enough, into the faint, basic lines that health and youth hadn't yet allowed to permanently mark the smoothness of her skin. But they were there now, those lines, and the brutality, sheathed over but evident, that showed in her close look towards him.

For the second time in the past days Cleve had the uncomfortable feeling that he knew Neila Willis exactly as she was. He didn't move or speak, letting the lash of her new words, livid and edgy, scrape over his nerves.

". . . You can have Harold. I'll toss him to your lions, Cleve, but — is that café girl so wonderful, you wouldn't throw her over — for me? I told you I loved you. All right; those are my terms. Leave the girl — forget her — and we'll go away together. You and me. I've got plenty of money."

She stopped speaking suddenly. The silence was broken by crickets singing drowsily in the warm evening. Cleve's spoken words sounded sullen. Actually, they weren't, but they were slowly said because he was on unfamiliar ground, to him. He knew she was dominating him, the conversation, even their thoughts and the atmosphere, there on the iron bench — and he didn't like it at all.

"Neila — there's something wrong with you. I'm sure of it. You —"

She interrupted, staring unblinkingly up at him. "I'm simply a woman, Cleve. Your little Cathy is something you'll tire of. She's soft and desirable and willing to bear your children and darn your socks. But you're not that type. I tell you you're not — you're a man!" The black eyes were dilated and fiery, flying signals of fury and a tempest of unleashed emotions that dwarfed them both. "You're strong and hard, Cleve. Hard and — cruel. And — I love you. That's all that matters."

She bent towards him, lips parted, eager and ready. Cleve didn't move. He felt the drumroll of raised emotions within him, his eyes were almost cold in their appraisal of her; then he got to his feet and stood before the bench looking down at her. The effect on the woman was like a slash across the face with a whip.

"Neila — I wouldn't trade Cathy for ten of you. You're sick — a little crazy, I think. From you I want just one thing. Your husband — where is he?"

Her face paled and remained rigid for a long second, then she looked up at him and made that mocking smile again. "You'd like to know, wouldn't you? You'd give a lot to know — almost anything — wouldn't you? Well — damn you, Cleve Simpson — you'll never find out!" The black eyes were twin shafts of deadly night cutting into his brain behind the eyes. "You won't unbend. I'm not so sure I want you now, after all. There's softness in you — not the cruelty I'd thought was there. I — don't think you've got guts after all. You're hollow inside, Cleve. Big and strong and beautiful outside, but gutless inside. All right — I've humbled myself to you, offered to sell Harold out, even. Now — it's changed. You'll never — never — find out where he is!"

He watched her get up quickly, stand very close to him for a long moment, then turn abruptly and walk away. He admired her grace, but felt a great surge of revulsion as he thought over how easily she would have sent her husband to his death. His mind conjured up an obscure, phantom-like shadow of Sam Lamarr's face. With the spectre came his anger. Sam was dead because of Harold Willis, but it was just as much Neila's fault, too.

He shrugged massive shoulders in the soft gloom of early evening, looking away, down over the wonderful languor of Jacksonville. His lips moved, and the words came out so softly he could scarcely hear them himself.

"As for Cathy — that's finished. You finished that too, Neila, and I owe you that score too. I don't have much more to lose, any more; just a life. I'll lose that too, Neila Willis, if I have to — *after* I see your husband and Ben Carter caught — and you set adrift a long way from Gold River!"

He turned and went back towards the little square, crude outline of a building in process of erection, unaware that the cloudiness of his eyes was like wood-smoke on an overcast day.

He didn't even see the men until Perc Overholt touched his arm.

"We looked high and low, Cleve — and found nothing."

"Well," Cleve said dully, "he's here somewhere. I know that, now."

Perc looked puzzled. "You see him — or something?"

"Neila Willis told me. I saw her; talked to her. They're both here."

"Carter too?"

Cleve shook his head. "No, I don't think so. Not from the way she talked. He hid out more'n likely. Might even have stayed over in Gold River."

Overholt swore dourly. "If he did, it was the last big mistake he'll ever make — the fool!"

There was a moment of silence while each man rambled through the maze of his own mind, then Overholt shrugged in dejection and looked up at Cleve again.

"Where the devil could Willis be, Cleve?"

Cleve's eyes narrowed slowly. "Neila was in the crowd around the building, boys. Willis won't be far away from his wife — you can count on that. She can't live in a barn loft like he can, so — unless they're living apart, which I don't believe — she should be able to lead us right to him."

89

"Sure — but where is she now?"

Cleve struck off towards the centre of the town. "We'll find out. She's not a plain woman. Men'll remember her passing by."

Overholt looked at Cleve and nodded gently. "Amen," he said softly.

They went to a saloon called the Territory. What held them there was a note nailed prominently to one wall. It had been folded and bore signs that it had come through the mail. It had attracted more than its share of attention too, for there were endless smudges from dirty fingers along it, underscoring the lines of words.

"I feel it my duty to the people of Jacksonville to warn them of the following condition, although I don't want to be known to you while doing it. Harold Willis, of Gold River, Oregon Territory, petitioned for the right to supervise erection of, as well as operation of, a branch mint and assay office in Jacksonville. This petition has been recently approved in Washington.

"Please be advised that Willis is doing this for dishonest purposes, and be cautioned and urgently advised against patronising his assay office.

"Further, I strongly urge the citizens

of Jacksonville to look into the integrity of your local head assayer, Mr. Owen Byrd, who has accepted a bribe from Willis.

"The writer sincerely suggests that you circumvent the doubtful and dishonest schemes of these two men.

"A Friend."

Perc turned slowly, gazing up at Cleve. "Now who in Hades wrote that?"

Cleve turned, saw the barkeep eyeing them, and went over to him. "Where did that thing come from?" he asked, pointing to the letter.

The man shrugged. "Darned if I know. It come in the post; that's all I can tell you."

Cleve nodded thoughtfully, looked back at Perc, and shrugged. "No telling, Perc; my guess is that Eric Schmidt or someone else over at Gold River wrote it, then sent it to Jacksonville, hoping to save the local miners from being taken in by Willis." He turned back to the barman, who was looking at the four men with open curiosity. "Pardner, you know a man named Harold Willis who comes from Gold River?"

"Only by name; why?"

"Well, would you know his wife if I described her to you?" Cleve suddenly asked.

"Naw," the man shook his head emphatically. He had lived to reach forty because his trade forbade telling what a man saw or heard or knew; he was looking forward to attaining twice that age by following the rule.

Cleve read it correctly before the man answered, and nodded to him. "All right; thanks." He left the saloon, stood on the duckboards lost in thought for a moment, then turned to the freckle-faced deputy town marshal with an intent look. "Fred, we've overlooked something; that letter in there'll help us even more than the writer intended."

"How?" the man asked bluntly.

"You go back in there and ask where Owen Byrd lives. He's a Willis man, and he'll know where Willis is," Cleve said, his eyes catching the glint of understanding in the deputy's features.

"Yeah," Perc added tritely. "If Byrd don't know, then we might as well go back to Gold River. We'll never find him over here without help — that's a gut."

The man went, and soon returned. Without a word, they trooped down the duckboards, their heavy boots making a dull, ominous sound in the gathering dusk. Eventually, they arrived before the modest, unpainted little bachelor household where the government man lived.

Cleve forced the door by himself. Byrd met

them in his small parlour, standing erect and ashen-white. He had the bulge of a gun under his coat, but he saw no chance to reach for it. Cleve took the gun from its holster and tossed it towards the fireplace at the far end of the room.

"Owen Byrd?"

"Yes. Who —"

"We'll ask the questions here. First, where's Harold Willis?"

"I don't know what you're —"

Perc's blow felled the man before he could finish the lie. He got slowly to his knees and looked up at them. There was a glint of terror on his suddenly pasty face.

Cleve jerked his head. "Get up; that's better. Now, once more — where's Willis?"

"All right, all right — I'll tell you. But — but what are you going to do?"

Cleve saw Overholt's movement and looked at the town marshal. Perc's hand encircled his throat slowly, tightened a little, then dropped away.

The assayer's eyes bulged. "No! Listen, I've done nothing." The man was abject. "With God as my witness, boys, I tell you that I never —"

"Listen, you yellow-bellied old buzzard," Overholt spat at him, "you're stalling. With God as *my* witness, you'll swing from the lamp bracket in your own ceiling if you don't answer — and the truth, too. *Where is Willis?*"

"Turlock — I mean the Turlock Hotel. Upstairs. I was with him this —"

"You're a liar," one of the deputies said. "We've been to that hotel and no one —"

"Not as Willis; he's listed under the name of Harry Rowell of San Francisco. Even has his meals sent up. He's no fool; you'll have to give him credit for that." Byrd's shoulders sagged. "He's —"

Cleve interrupted coldly. "Yeah, he's clever, all right; real clever, usually — but this time he's made a slip. His wife is wandering around loose in town."

Byrd's myopic eyes hung on Cleve's unshaven, lined face for a dawning second, then dropped away. "Of course," he said, "of course. That's how you found out he was here. Oh — she's just a fool."

"Yeah," Overholt said dryly. "And he's a fool for letting her run loose, too. If we hadn't seen her, we might've gone back to Gold River." He studied Byrd's stooped frame thoughtfully, then nodded to the sullen, murderous-looking deputy marshal who stood off to one side. "Stay here with this renegade, Jeb. Don't let him out of your sight. Wait here until we bring the horses back."

The deputy nodded easily, and motioned Byrd to a chair. He waited briefly until the

94

others had left, then swung back and glowered at his prisoner with a savage look that promised direct and prompt violence if the assayer moved.

Byrd understood it easily enough; he watched the deputy marshal sink into a deep, overstuffed rocker and settle back. He wished with all the power of his being that he had never laid eyes on Harold Willis.

CHAPTER FOUR

Outwitted

The pimply-faced clerk at the Turlock Hotel looked at the three men crossing the tiny lobby towards him. He sniffed his annoyance at the sight of the freckled man — he had been there before. It was the cold look on Cleve's face that made him stiffen uneasily as the men ranged themselves in front of him.

Cleve reached over, spun the ledger, and ran a finger down the columns until he came to the name of Harry Rowell. His grey eyes raised to the clerk and held him. "Where is this man?"

A quick glance at Rowell's signature, and the pimply face lightened its shade. "I — suppose — he's upstairs."

"And his wife?"

"Wife?" The clerk's eyebrows shot upwards in bewilderment.

"Yes — wife. Black-eyed, black-haired woman," Cleve said.

The clerk started. "Oh; she's his wife? Well —" his mind was obviously resurrecting Neila

96

and admiring her. "She — isn't here."

"No?" Its softness was lethal. The clerk writhed under the implication and looked into each face. There was plain destruction visible in each set of grim eyes.

He shrugged finally. "She — just came in a little while ago."

"They're both upstairs?"

"Yeah. Yes."

"Any visitors with them?"

"No; if there are, I didn't see them go up."

Cleve was wondering where Neila had been if she had just gone upstairs to her husband's room. He turned to the freckled deputy town marshal. "Stay here, will you, Fred? We'll go up, but we'd just as soon have our backs protected, too. If Carter, or anyone else that you don't like the looks of, comes in, just hold 'em here until we come down with our prisoner."

Fred smiled boyishly. "Sure; I'll be here. Won't nobody get up them stairs, either, if they look at all funny to me." He shook his head vigorously.

Perc Overholt turned away swiftly and mounted the stairs. Cleve was close behind, his right hand buried in his trousers pocket, curled around the .41 under-and-over Derringer he carried. The sounds of Jacksonville's pleasant night came to them through the

97

opened windows of the hotel, and through the paper-thin walls as well; then they were on the hallway planking itself, turning left down the dimly-lit corridor.

Perc touched Cleve's arm. His face was anxious in the semi-gloom. "Where in Hades are they? The darned clerk didn't say."

Cleve looked a little irritated and thoroughly villainous in the weak light. Without answering, he shouldered past Perc and began slowly stalking down the dingy hall, halting at each closed door to listen at the panel. It wasn't until he was near a door that led down into the roadway from the end of the hall by a night entrance that he heard what he was listening for — familiar voices. He smiled coldly at Perc; the marshal drew his gun and stepped a little to one side, then nodded.

Cleve had the Derringer in his big fist when the voice behind them spoke so softly that they barely heard it. "Hold it, boys. Freeze!"

A thin, bony hand reached over and snatched their guns away; then the man faced them. He was a moose in size, with small, cruel eyes and strangely delicate, extremely long-fingered hands. The little eyes blinked over them, then fastened on Cleve's face.

"You must be Simpson." The sardonic laugh was as dry as corn husks in the wind. "Hard to kill, ain't you?"

The man was a stranger to Cleve. "Who are you, and what's the idea —"

"Neila got to me about an hour ago. I come back to — sort of wait for you, like she said."

Cleve nodded gently. Neila hadn't really believed that he wouldn't find her husband. Then she'd known it all along, and provided this gunman to stop him when he did. He appraised the man coldly. "You got a price, hombre?"

The man shook his head with a wolfish grin. "Sure, but *you* can't pay it." The man moved warily around Cleve, keeping his cocked six-gun low and steady. He was reaching blindly behind him for Willis's door when Perc Overholt kicked out viciously, desperately, with a scuffed boot.

The gunman was caught in the side with terrific force; he went sideways with an animal scream of agony and squeezed off a shot that jarred the rear entrance door loose on its hinges. Then Cleve was on him like a madman, beating him into unconsciousness with big fists that flailed into his twisted face.

Cleve heard Perc shout something from a long way off. Then a gun exploded, quickly followed by two fast shots and the sound of rushing feet.

Cleve jumped off the man, snatched up the .44 he had seen fall to the floor, and whirled.

Cleve saw just a single flash of Neila flying down the stairs, then there were only two men near him, and Perc Overholt was holding a bloody hand with a look in his eyes of dumbfounded disbelief.

Cleve's fury died slowly. He pocketed the .44 and went to Perc. "Bad?"

The word seemed to jar Overholt back into reality. He shook himself and squinted at the gore, shaking his head. "No, and it's my left hand at that. God Almighty, but that happened fast."

Cleve watched Perc fashion a make-shift bandage of sorts over the deep score of Willis's wild shot. "Exactly what happened, Perc?"

The town marshal shot a vengeful glance at the man lying awkwardly nearby before he answered. "Him, there — that whelp — let 'em know what was up. I was moving around to skull-crack him when they both come out. I seen Willis and sent off two fast ones, but I know they were wide, because he just faced me and fired. Then they both run to the stairs and got clean away."

Cleve looked at the bulky bandages, turned away quickly, and ran through the room that Willis and his wife had occupied to the window in front of the building. The people he sought were nowhere in sight, but he did see the pimply-faced clerk running toward the hotel at the head of several men wearing badges.

He grunted and went back to Perc. "Come on, we're about to be cornered by the sheriff — or someone."

"Where to?"

Cleve was moving fast when he answered. "Out this night entrance."

They made it easily and stood back in a dingy alley where visibility was nil, resting and rearranging Perc's sloppy, crude-looking bandages.

Cleve's attention was jerked violently away from Perc at the sound of footsteps clattering down the night entrance steps. His burly hand automatically reached for the .44 he had taken from the man who lay unconscious on the floor outside of Willis's empty room. A thin smile washed over his face as he saw Jeb, the murderous look still in his eyes, swing into the alley.

"Jeb; over here!" Cleve waited until the deputy town marshal had come up close, then he asked, "Did you get them?"

"Get who?" Jeb asked.

"Willis and his wife."

"Nobody came down the front way," Jeb answered. "I heard gunshots, and I come upstairs just in time to see you going out the back way."

Cleve nodded. "Then the Willises must have

come out the night entrance, too. Well," he shrugged helplessly, "it's too late to catch them now."

"Cleve, I could've shot her," Perc said quietly.

"I expect you should have, really; she's absolutely no good. In some ways she's worse than her husband."

Overholt's eyes widened. "But aren't you in love with her?"

"What! Where in Hades you get that idea, Perc?"

Overholt shrugged in embarrassment. "Well, dammit — Cathy told me you was in love with Neila Willis when I saw her last night after the damned fire. She was plumb sick over it, too, Cleve." He moved off in the darkness. The last words came mumbled, like an apology, which they weren't. "It's none of my business, of course — and I know it. Come on."

Cleve fell in beside Perc and said nothing for a long time. It was not until they emerged from the gloom of the alley into the southern section of town and saw the livery barn across the road from where they stood that Cleve spoke. "Perc, Cathy's wrong as she can be; she saw me with Neila at my shack. Since then she's been steering clear of me. I don't love Neila, and never did, Perc. I love Cathy

102

Brittan and I asked her to marry me."

Perc looked at him in surprise. "Hell, Cleve, I don't reckon you made it very clear then, because she told me you was in love with —"

"Forget it," Cleve snapped. "I'll get the horses while you fetch your deputies and we'll head down through town. Unless I'm way off, Willis won't stay in Jacksonville now, either."

"Where'll he go?"

Cleve shrugged. "I'm gambling that the liveryman'll have an idea. I don't. See you later."

Perc went scuffling off in the semi-gloom, looking askance at his throbbing hand and wagging his head back and forth over the puzzle of strange behaviour that had overcome Cleve and Cathy. How two people who loved each other could be so far apart was a mystery to Perc Overholt.

Cleve nailed the nighthawk. "Did a man and woman come in here within the last half hour or so?"

"You must mean this Roswell hombre and that black-headed witch of his."

The description stopped Cleve cold. He considered it for a second, then nodded brusquely. "That's righter than you know, pardner."

"Yeah; they come in, got a rig, and left. Real funny, too. The rig just come in with the doc. I was taking the horse out of the shafts when they both come in, slipped me a gold piece, and had me put the horse back and let 'em have it." His head wagged in bewilderment.

"Yes," Cleve agreed mirthlessly, "very funny. Tell me something, was that horse tired?"

"Naw," the liveryman frowned. "Doc don't use no animal hard. Mostly he goes places and leaves his horse standing under a tree while —"

"Which way did the man and woman drive out — or didn't you see?"

The hostler eyed Cleve critically, speculatively, then shrugged expressively. "Pardner, there ain't no woman in Jacksonville like Roswell's woman. Of course I looked; they went south, toward Gold River."

Cleve turned away quickly, found the horses of his own party, and began saddling and bridling them. The hostler watched until he knew what was happening, then pitched in to help Cleve. He caught the gold piece that Cleve flung to him and stood back to watch as Cleve swung up and rode out. The hostler shook his head dolefully at the stranger who was leading the three horses, and smiled thinly at the glint in Cleve's eyes.

Cleve was a hundred yards from the barn's entrance when the darkness opened up and lashed out at him in an orange tongue of flame. He could feel his horse quiver violently from the sudden impact for the space of a brief second, then it collapsed without taking another step. The reins of the led animals were yanked savagely out of his hand, but he was dragged clear of the downed animal and landed in the thick, swirling dust of the roadway before the second mushroom of orange flame crashed into the darkness, sending the three saddled horses trotting back toward the barn, heads held high and sideways, dragging their reins in the dust as they went.

Cleve twisted and rolled back to the warm, sleek hulk of his dead animal. He fished in his pocket and came up with his .44. Someone shouted farther uptown. The sound came to him and he interpreted it as meaning nothing more than possibly more trouble. Then he was searching narrow-lidded for his attacker.

There was a musical sound of spurred boots in a narrow declivity between two stores. Cleve aimed at the sound and fired. Someone swore in a yelping, high voice. Cleve felt slight satisfaction; he hadn't hit the man, but he had shown that Cleve Simpson wasn't downed either. He recalled the man he had left unconscious in the hotel and made a dour face. He should have killed him when he had the chance.

Another shot blasted. Cleve fired instantly at the tongue of flame, heard a guttural grunt, and fired again. There was a vicious explosion off to one side of him uptown. Startled, he turned a little when a slug ploughed into the inert form of his cooling bulwark with a sickening, ripping sound.

A shadow loomed up drunkenly where he had fired at the first man. He glanced back swiftly, saw the man holding his chest with arms strangely stiff and out-flung with elbows bent double. The .44 was poised, but Cleve knew the man would never fire again.

Fascinated, Cleve watched the silhouette come out from between the buildings, weave blindly up the duckboards toward the centre of town for a good hundred feet, then one spurted boot missed its timing and the stricken man went down in a sprawling fall that resembled a felled tree and lay there half on the duckboards and half in the gutter.

Cleve's exultation was bitter and short-lived. He knew that there were two men and he also knew that Neila Willis had kept her word. She had friends in Jacksonville who would sell their lives readily at her slightest whim. One had already done so — another was willing to.

He twisted back, lowering his glance to find the other hidden killer. Men were yelling at one another farther up the road. They came vaguely into focus, but a hesitant reluctance kept them from approaching too closely to the dark lump in the road that was Cleve Simpson and his dead horse.

Two fast shots roiled the thick dust and sprayed filth over him, but Cleve had already re-loaded and was ready. He pin-pointed the gunman and fired three times as fast as he could straddle the gunflash with two shots and drive the third one directly between the other two. The hidden killer swore loudly and scratchily; he was hit hard.

Cleve was altogether surprised when the man jumped out of the dark and raced at him, slashing the gloom with gunfire that seared into his eyeballs with its brilliance. Holding his gun level, Cleve thought that any friend of Neila Willis would have to be such a man; fearless, brutal and violent.

He saw the thick chest and fired. The man stopped in mid-stride, then staggered back a step on rubbery legs. Cleve's final shot dropped him flat on his back in the swirling dust.

The silence closed in again on Cleve's little patch of world. He lay there relaxed but uncertain until a shout came to him from the men up the road. "You there, behind the horse, you hit?"

"No," Cleve answered evenly. "Not yet."

"Well, stand up, will you?"

Cleve didn't answer; he was pretty certain that there had been only two of them, but he wasn't going to stand up and make a target out of himself to be certain.

"All right — hold your fire; I'm coming to you."

Cleve squirmed around and watched the tall, burly man come alone through the shadows. He saw the reflected glint of metal on the man's chest and sighed.

"All right, constable, I see you, so you can put up the gun."

The big man stopped about ten feet away and was leaning forward a little from the waist, trying to pierce the darkness with his glance. He grunted abruptly and looked around at the two dead men, raked over the buildings with his eyes, then slowly, reluctantly holstered his gun and walked closer. He nodded. "If there was any more, they been scairt off. You can get up, I think."

Cleve pushed himself out of the dirt, looked broodingly at the dead horse, and began to brush the sticky dust off his already mussed and filthy clothing.

The constable appraised him critically. "No hurts?"

"Nope."

"Who in hell jumped you?"

Cleve shrugged and shook his head, looking past the big man at the bodies. He said nothing.

The constable turned stiffly and walked to the nearest dead man and toed him a little with a boot toe. The words came pensively to Cleve. "Joe Martin; well — he was never no good, anyhow. Damned renegade." The lawman went to the other man and squinted closer at him, then straightened, turned, and went back to Cleve. "What's your name, mister?"

"Cleve Simpson; I'm from Gold River."

"Well, Cleve Simpson, you shot two men tonight. One," he waved an indifferent hand toward the farthest body, "was Joe Martin. He never was no good. But, dammit, this other one's Marty Sage."

Cleve looked inquiringly at the lawman. "Who's he?"

"One of my deputies."

Cleve nodded more to himself than to the town constable of Jacksonville. Neila would attract many kinds — good and bad. "This Joe Martin; is he a tall, husky hombre with skinny hands and pale eyes?"

The lawman nodded shortly, looking straight at Cleve. "Yeah; you met him before?"

Cleve inclined his head. "Yeah," he said dryly. "He threw down on me once before tonight." A melancholy was settling over Cleve. He slowly punched out the spent shells and re-loaded the .44, dropped it into his coat pocket, and patted the pocket. "I took this gun away from him earlier."

"Yeah? Was that in the Turlock Hotel?" the lawman asked.

Cleve nodded.

The constable scratched his ribs vigorously, squinting. "Well, hell; the clerk got me and the boys to go over there. Nobody there when we went up, but plenty of blood. What happened?"

Cleve shrugged. The urgency he had felt to pursue the Willises was draining out of him; weariness was taking its place. "This feller Martin jumped a friend of mine and me. We downed him and took his gun away. That's about all there was to it."

"What was it about?"

Again Cleve shrugged. "Just a little personal difference, is all."

The constable nodded slightly. "This here was sort of personal, too, I reckon. What in Hades got into my deputy to make him jump you like that? You know?"

"No; I've got no idea. Maybe he was put up to it."

110

"Yeah," the lawman said, unconvinced and still greatly puzzled. "Well — it was a fair fight. Most of the town seen it, too." The man's face turned down toward the dead men briefly, then swung back to Cleve. "Was you going back to Gold River when they jumped you?"

"I reckon."

"All right. You live over there?" The constable watched Cleve nod assent. "Well, I don't know whether I'll need you again or not; that's up to the coroner. I doubt it, though. It was plain self-defence. Anyway, if you're around for a while, it'd sort of help, maybe. Y'know, in case anything comes of this."

Cleve smiled wanly. "I'll be around, don't worry about that; I'm mayor of Gold River."

The lawman's indecision vanished like magic. He even managed a tight little grin. "Oh, well — in that case, it's different. Glad to know you, Mister Simpson." He offered a hand that Cleve shook. "You're free to go when you want to." The shaken hand waved toward the dead horse. "I'll take care of that for you."

Cleve was fortunate in that the liveryman had a good chestnut gelding for sale cheap. He bought the animal, transferred his gear, and took the reins of the other three horses again. Cleve rode past his own dead horse, sprawled and peaceful-looking in the dim light, and gazed briefly at the dead men.

Cleve arrived at Owen Byrd's place and had the deputy who was standing guard mount their prisoner behind him. The assayer was too shaken to protest, but the deputy who owned the horse grumbled a little under his breath.

Jacksonville was alive with interest, for the news of the sudden assault and its abrupt termination in two deaths was passed from mouth to mouth through the normally quiet, sleepy little town.

Later, when Perc Overholt and his deputies were heading back toward the open country beside Cleve, the town marshal asked about the shooting he had heard. Perc was astounded at Cleve's recitation of the attack. He screwed up his face thoughtfully and stared ahead into the night. "Then that slows us up on the Willises. Where do you reckon they'd go? Surely not to Gold River."

"Why not, Perc? Dangerous, sure — but don't forget that they got a safe full of money over there. Besides, as far as they know, Neila's gunmen should've finished me, which'd give them plenty of time to slip in, loot the place, and make their getaway." The more Cleve thought about it, the more plausible it sounded in his own mind. Especially since he knew Harold Willis to be a man to whom risk meant comparatively little in comparison to solid and substantial gain.

Overholt swore at the ground and shook his head. "If it was daylight, we could track 'em — maybe."

The freckled deputy shot a glance at him. "Not likely; at least, not in summer, Perc."

Cleve shrugged. "If we don't catch 'em, it won't be anything we can't live without, I reckon."

"No," Perc shot back. "But for Sam's sake, I'd like to see Willis hanging from a limb."

"Sure, Perc; I would, too," Cleve answered. "And there's a good chance we would've, if I hadn't been waylaid in Jacksonville. But if we don't, at least we've done what we set out to do; clean up Gold River." He nodded in the darkness, gently. "And I reckon Sam'd settle for that first, and the Willises second. Anyway, Neila told me that Carter stayed at Gold River."

"The hell!" Perc said explosively, squinting at the husky man beside him. "Well! I thought he was with Willis."

"No; at least, Neila said not. I expect he's hiding out at Gold River — if he's there."

"Yeah," the dark, sullen-looking deputy said dourly. "If he ain't left by now."

Cleve said no more. They rode at a good clip, although they did not push their animals. Each man felt sure that the Willises would go to Gold River, but none of them believed they would still be there when they rode into town.

CHAPTER FIVE

Hangrope Justice

Cleve Simpson saw the great bonfire first. He leaned forward a little, concentrating his attention on it. A few seconds later, the others saw and gasped.

Perc Overholt swore excitedly. "What's happened now? The fire was out when we left."

"No," Cleve said slowly. "That's a bonfire, Perc. Must be having a rally."

They rode closer, near enough to see the milling throng of humanity writhing like spectres in the alternating flashes of sordid light then darkness. Cleve had a premonition. He felt it at the jerky, unreal way the host of miners were acting and spurred his horse into a lope that brought him in among the throng that fell silent at his approach.

Eric Schmidt came out of the sweating press of men. His heavy-featured, slightly brutish face was shiny with sweat. There was a faint showing of uneasiness — almost to the point of embarrassment — in his eyes as he looked up and waited for Cleve to speak.

"Why did you do it, Eric?"

Schmidt turned slowly, raised his eyes to the object that Cleve looked away from. The body twisted slowly, limply, from the lariat rope that held it to the limb in the back of the bonfire. Ben Carter was dead — lynched. The others had ridden up and were transfixed at horror at the spectacle of the lolling tongue and bulging eyes outlined in awful, shifting shadows that highlighted the bloated face. It looked indescribably evil.

Eric spread his massive hands before him, looking a little to one side of Cleve's face. "He run for it. We commenced searching for him after you left. One of the boys said he'd seen Carter in town this morning. The damned fool jumped on a tied horse out back of the Gold River House and ran for it. I tried like hell, Cleve, but they wouldn't stop. Even after they brung him back, I tried to save him for a trial. I told 'em that's what we was fighting against: lawlessness and violence. They wouldn't listen." Eric shrugged expressive shoulders. "All right, Cleve; I tried. It wasn't no use."

"So you joined 'em," Cleve said dryly.

Eric nodded. "Yeah, so I joined 'em. Cleve, he had it coming — and worse — the —"

"I know," Cleve said simply. "But he should have been saved for a trial. Even he was entitled to a trial, Eric; he should've been saved."

"Sure; I honestly tried, Cleve; by God, I did."

The crowd was sobering rapidly. Some of the more sensitive miners were already finding solace in the shadows. Cleve looked at them and he was a little disillusioned. His words carried evenly although he didn't raise his voice. Eric Schmidt didn't flinch under them, but a lot of other men did.

"That's the way wolves do it. Carter himself would've done it that way. Carter and Willis. We want things to be different from the way animals do things — that's why we got into this battle with Willis's outfit in the first place." He tilted his head briefly at the dead man. "A thing like this makes us no better than Willis or Carter."

A fiery-eyed young miner with whisky-inflamed eyes glared at Cleve. "We got our man; where's yours? Where's Willis?" His eyes swept around. "Who's riding double? It ain't Willis."

Eric turned to the man, but Perc Overholt beat him to it. "Shut your mouth!" The man subsided, sobered a little by the formidable venom of Eric and Perc.

Cleve turned to the town marshal. "Perc, I reckon you're the whole shebang now. Sheriff and town marshal. You're the whole law in Gold River. You have Byrd; lock him up somewhere, will you?"

Perc nodded, sitting his horse like a wizened scarecrow; cold, dirty and satanic-looking in the fading glow, staring out of bitter eyes at the thinning crowd. "All right; what's first — after cutting Carter down, I mean?"

"Willis," Cleve said curtly.

"What you got in mind?"

"I reckon we'd better organise a posse. Eric'll help you. Put riders out in every direction, Perc, and post a regular cordon around Gold River. If he's gone on through, well — we'll probably never get him. If he hasn't — if he's still to come — we can catch him coming in, maybe, or after he gets here."

Perc nodded, looked speculatively at Eric Schmidt, then he swung down off his horse and gingerly tested his saddle-bowed legs.

Cleve reined away from the sickening sight, rode over to a hitch-rail, swung down and faced a young miner with a worried look. "Pardner, will you take this horse to the liverybarn and tell the nighthawk that it isn't the horse I rented from him, but to keep it until I get down there? Tell him I'll explain then."

"Sure, Cleve," the man said, relieved. "Be glad to."

The weariness was closing in again, like lead

in his veins. He went down the plankwalk automatically until he got to Cathy's café. The place was dark and silent. He tried the door, found it locked, and knocked heavily on the panel with a grimy fist. The sound rattled hollowly through the little building, and its echo was interrupted by the next pounding, more insistent than the first.

"Who is it?"

"Cathy; it's me, Cleve Simpson."

"Oh." A moment's silence. "What do you want?"

"I want to talk to you."

"All right; I'm listening."

Cleve felt a touch of initiation, then it died down suddenly when he thought that in her eyes, at least, he deserved the treatment he was getting.

"Not through the door, Cathy; I can't say what I have to say to a plank."

"You'll get as much consideration from the door as you'll get from me," she answered caustically.

Cleve's indignation grew. His emotions were frayed from the assaults of the night. It told in his voice, too, when he spoke again. "Listen, Cathy; maybe you think I deserve this. Well, I don't. If you won't give me a chance to explain what happened, then I'll kick the door down and make you listen."

She heard the stubborn anger in his tone and was startled by it. For a moment, she didn't answer. "All right; just a minute."

The door opened reluctantly and Cathy's small, pretty oval of a face showed before him, apprehension written into the corners of her eyes and the set of her mouth. She was wearing a clinging wrapper over her nightdress.

"Cathy, Neila came to the shack to see if a gunman Willis had sicked on me had actually done the job. He hadn't, and I waylaid her. She — I don't know how to explain it, and I don't think you'd understand it if I do. I'm not sure that I'm right, anyway — but she's got some kind of quirk."

"Yes; hasn't she?" Cathy said with of flash of savagery in her eyes and voice that stunned Cleve for a second. It was a little of the same primitiveness that he had seen in Neila. The identical basis in fury, but more subdued, perhaps. Cleve felt an unconscious antagonism in reaction that thrilled to her flash of passion.

"I'm trying to tell you, Cathy —"

Cathy's eyes were filmed with a sort of sheen of desperation. "Cleve, why are you lying to me?"

"I'm not lying," he answered furiously. "You're blind; that's all. You don't want to believe me, Cathy. You got a glimpse of something sordid — and it was sordid, all of it

— and you're giving it a warped interpretation. For some reason, you're torturing yourself with what you saw, with what you must know deep inside wasn't — isn't — the truth."

She laughed shortly, harshly, and tossed her head a little. "Torturing myself? Why would I do that? Do you think I care enough to —"

"No, I don't, Cathy." The words were dammed up behind his teeth. He held them there in a battle with his anger. The breath came slowly, like a sigh, past his lips, and he slouched a little, looking at the fullness of her. His voice changed when he spoke again; it was dry and tired. "Listen, Cathy; I love you and I have for a long time. Please, what can I say? Neila Willis is evil to me. I don't want to fight with you, darling. I don't want to argue. I want you to understand that I'm not lying to you, Cathy. I won't lie to you." There he held back the flood of words again, fearing to mar what he had said with more, and looked at her.

For several impassive moments, Cathy looked into his face, unmoving in expression. Then the anguish seeped in around her blue eyes and made her face a little ugly. "Cleve, I want to believe you; I've always wanted to."

"Then — why don't you?"

She made a small, furtive little gesture with one hand. "I've been around miners — rough

121

men — all my life. Don't forget, I sleep here at the café at night. I see men by day that are completely changed when they come into Gold River from their shacks at night. They're — almost like animals, Cleve. Ever since I was a little girl, I've seen these two sides of men. I don't fear them exactly, Cleve, but I — don't trust them, either."

"I see; I'm a man — just like the others — to you. Is that it, Cathy?"

She shook her head a little, gently. "No; you never have been. That's why I crawled out of my shell a little, when you said — you like me. I watched you, and I wondered. You didn't have a Chileño, Cleve; you didn't go to the Gold River House after dark and go wild like the others."

"But still — you were afraid, is that it?"

Cathy nodded mutely, watching him, seeing the dead colour of his flesh and the sagging, greasy look of its exhaustion. It hurt her to see him like that and know she was adding to his burden.

"And you saw Neila Willis — a woman you don't understand — in my cabin at dawn." He spoke softly, but brutally, leaning against the door jamb against the weariness that even in this moment of passion threatened to overcome him. "And you ran back into your shell again." He shook his head at her. "Cathy, please; I don't want to argue with you about it. All I want you to know is that there never was anything between Neila Willis and me — no matter what you saw — and that I want you to marry me. I can't promise you much, darling, but you'll never have to be afraid of me being unfaithful or unfair to you."

She was holding the door. In the dying light he could see her fingernails grinding at the wood. The tendons stood out in all their straining might, then Cleve straightened and went toward her. She didn't move away until he was very close; then she went sideways a little, drawing him inward. She gave the door a shove with her hand, waiting for him in the darkness that swallowed them up.

Cleve could feel her quivering and held her close. The uneven, dull tumult of her heart-beats broke against his chest and he brought his head down a little and found her mouth. There were tears, salty and warm, on his lips.

She was pulling him to her, letting the confined juices she had held in so long have free rein, racking her body until she could no longer hold back the spasms that shook her.

Cleve knew the peace that was overcoming him was what he had longed for, lived for, and, secretly, what had motivated him from the start in the fight to make Gold River a decent place for a woman and a man's family.

He was holding her to him, refreshed and absorbing the energy from her, when the night went apart in a searing explosion that shook the café like it was made of cardboard. They came apart in violent astonishment, uncomprehending and perfectly motionless until Cleve heard the hoarse shouts of men in the road.

He turned back to Cathy and held her close. "Say you'll marry me, Cathy; quick."

"I'll marry you, Cleve. I — love you."

He smiled for the first time that night, squeezed her shoulders, bent a little and kissed the triangle at the base of her throat, then straightened. "Stay inside, darling. I'll be back."

Then he was gone and the door slammed gratingly behind him, leaving her there in the darkness, spent and weak, listening to someone call his name in excitement outside.

"Cleve! It's the Gold River House — look!"

He heard the man but didn't listen. The panorama of ruin was settling. Dust hung like a high shroud over the place. The explosion had shattered both buildings flanking the saloon and had blown out lanterns on the opposite side of the road, torn down fences and scattered loose objects for hundreds of feet.

The Gold River House had been dynamited. It hung in an awry, settling position, gutted inside but not burning, shattered so that only the shell still stood, and that creaked ominously as though it might crash inward upon itself at any second.

Cleve felt rather than saw Perc Overholt and Eric Schmidt beside him, standing as he was, aghast at the devastation and held spellbound by the huge buildings' great dust and smaller sounds.

"Eric, who did it?"

Eric spoke in the silence and stillness that followed the question. Men were gathered nearby; some went in close, gaping at the devastation. "I don't have no idea."

Cleve recovered and faced Eric. "Was it some of the miners, you reckon?"

The thick-set man shook his head adamantly. "No, I'll bet my life on it. They was pretty ashamed over Carter — all of 'em. No," he shook his head, "I'll take an oath on it, Cleve."

Perc was fashioning a cigarette with shaky fingers. He fell back into his habit of swearing without reason, blindly, when he was upset, then he shook his head and twisted his face up. "Well, it was a good job, only whoever done it didn't start no fire this time, like I expect they hoped would happen."

Cleve nodded quickly. "That's it, Perc; that's it sure as hell."

"What?" Perc asked, looking at Cleve from behind the bluish smoke with a puzzled expression.

"Willis; I should've guessed it before; he turned the wagon loose that killed Sam, didn't he?"

"Well," Eric said heavily, "we don't know. It might've been Carter. He never told us, though."

Cleve frowned. "I don't mean that Willis gave the wagon the first shove, Eric; I mean that he was behind the thing. He had to be. He was the leader of the opposition. It was Willis's idea, I mean." He jerked his head at the Gold River House. "So was this; it's the same kind of thinking. Blow it up, using dynamite."

Perc was staring. "That means he's close by; maybe he even went up with the saloon."

Eric snorted. "Not Willis, Perc; he ain't tired of living — not that hombre."

Cleve saw the men in the crowd getting more reckless. He nodded to them, where they were edging up for a peek inside the gutted building. "Darned fools. Perc, get your deputies; rope the place off. It'll cave in, more'n likely."

"Yeah, but —"

"Don't worry; I'll get some men. Eric, here, will go with me. If the Willises are still in

126

this country, we'll find 'em."

Eric nodded. "Sure; they'll play hell getting through them out-riders, anyway."

Perc watched Eric and Cleve trot in ungainly haste toward the liverybarn, shrugged irritably, and looked through the throng for his deputies.

When they were mounted, Cleve turned to Eric with a thin scowl. "Eric, we'll do better if we split up."

"How you mean?"

Cleve waved his arm southward, in the general direction of Jacksonville. "They may've blown up the saloon like we figure, after coming back in the night and getting their money, or whatever they came back for. That was our blunder. We put guards all around Gold River and completely forgot to stake men out at the Gold River House. All right; now they're riding. They may darned well have headed back toward Jacksonville. I don't know, it's just a hunch. You take what guards you can find that're stationed outside of town and comb hell out of the countryside. Don't let 'em get away agin, Eric."

The miner nodded shortly. "And you; where are you going?"

"I'm going to do the same thing northward. We'll both make a half-circle so's Gold River's got a complete circle around it. If they're here, we ought to find 'em — one of us." Cleve's eyes focused on the miner. "Eric, we want the Willises alive — remember that."

Schmidt winced and gathered the reins without looking at Cleve. "All right; see you later."

Cleve didn't wait. He turned his horse and rode northward out of Gold River, pounding into the night. Two men had died already in this town because of a deadly man and his strange, evil wife. One, a hero; the other, a catspaw whose own meagre intelligence had led him blindly down a trail that a smarter man might have known, days before, could end but one way — in death.

The predawn chill seeped through Cleve's filthy clothing, still bearing the manured dust of the road in Jacksonville where two strangers had died, too; unknowing and perhaps unwitting victims of Harold Willis's shattered plans of empire.

A man's flinty voice flashed out of the night and a rider loomed up, rifle cocked and shouldered, holding Cleve steady in the sights. "Hold it, hombre! Right where you are — Cleve?"

"Yeah, it's me. Somebody blew up the Gold River House. We were out —"

"By gawd," the man blurted, shaken. "I heard the noise. It — seemed like thunder out here." The enormity of the act soaked in

128

slowly. "Who done it?"

Cleve wagged his head impatiently. "We don't know. Figure it might've been the Willises. Eric's picking up the mounted men south of town and I want the riders north of town to form into a posse. We're going to patrol the countryside. If it was the Willises, we've got to get them."

The man was shaking his head in a short, emphatic wag. "Ain't been a soul come by here. Not a soul — until you come up."

Cleve whirled his horse. "All right, let's hunt up the others. We can't waste time."

The guard led out in a high lope that carried them forward, where other men were watching them come up, their stubbled faces blurs in the pale light. It didn't take long. Cleve had his posse and as they rode he singled out the men whose claims were in the surrounding woods to act as guides.

They scoured the woods and countryside until they met Eric's men, then retraced their steps, letting the new day break over them in an awesome panorama of mauve and grey that presaged rain.

It was close to seven o' clock before Cleve admitted defeat and dismissed the miners. In town he met Perc Overholt, who was talking to two well-dressed strangers in evident uneasiness.

129

The *pro tem.* sheriff was relieved and beckoned rapidly when Cleve rode up and swung down. "Cleve, this here's a United States Marshal."

The Federal man smiled and extended a hand. He was as tall as Cleve, but he lacked about thirty pounds of the mayor's weight. "Name's Hendricks, Mr. Simpson."

Cleve shook hands and returned the smile. Hendricks turned to the man with him. "This is Territorial Commissioner Andrew Stevens, Mr. Simpson." Again Cleve shook and smiled.

Perc looked a little worried. "Cleve, they come up about the trouble at Jacksonville. Seems the Commissioner got word from the town marshal at Jacksonville that you killed them hombres that jumped you over there, and this U.S. Marshal just come in and the Commissioner brought him along." Perc looked a little deferentially at the two men. "Isn't that about it, gentlemen?"

"Right, Mr. Overholt, thanks." The marshal turned to Cleve, studying him closely. "The sheriff's been telling us of your difficulties in Gold River. Frankly, some of the rumours have already reached San Francisco. That's how I happened to be at the Territorial capital for presentation of credentials before I came here when Commissioner Stevens was about to come down."

130

Cleve nodded. "There isn't much to tell now, except that the Willises have gotten away."

Perc grunted painfully. "No sign, Cleve?"

"No, none at all. It's a mystery to me how they got clear of Gold River like they did."

Commissioner Stevens had said nothing until now. He studied Cleve carefully before he said, "I'm sorry to hear that; it's unfortunate, but I feel that the apprehension of these people isn't the main stake here." Cleve listened, saying nothing. "I believe the important thing is to get the branch mint and assay office established is quickly as possible. Obviously, the need is urgent. Mister Simpson, you're the mayor here, aren't you?"

Perc nodded quickly. "Yes, sir, he is."

"Yes; well, wouldn't it be sensible if you went before the Territorial Legislature and told the facts that has kept this area in a turmoil for the past few months?"

Cleve thought it over. "What good would that do?"

"Well," Stevens said blandly, "I believe the petition granted Willis can be transferred by Territorial judiciary power, acting for the States government, to a miners' committee such as you men have in operation here." The Commissioner smiled slightly. "Or, if that's too radical, I'm equally positive

131

a director of the miners' choosing can be appointed for this branch mint. The thing is simply this: we don't want to delay the mint's operation any longer than possible for fear that this disorder will continue — and maybe spread."

Perc Overholt turned on his heel and walked swiftly away. The U.S. Marshal and the Commissioner looked after him a little dumbfounded.

Cleve smiled at them. "Perc has something on his mind. His prisoner, maybe; please excuse him."

Hendricks nodded. "Certainly, we've already talked to Mister Byrd." The capable mouth pulled downwards a little. "His primary concern seems to be that we save him from what happened to this Carter fellow."

Cleve nodded. "That was too bad." He shook his head dolefully. "Not that Carter didn't have it coming but it was just the way they —"

"Of course," Hendricks said. "We understand. In a sense, you can't blame a mob, sometimes. This was one of those times."

"I'm glad you feel that way. Frankly, I've been a little worried about the effect of Carter's lynching on gaining recognition and help from the Territorial people and the Federal government."

132

Hendricks spread his hands palm downward. "No reason to worry there."

The Commissioner cleared his throat. "Gentlemen, I think the sheriff had something pressing on his mind." They followed the man's glance and saw Overholt, Eric Schmidt and the other members of the miners' committee converging on them, along with a hastily summoned group of men who came from the general direction of the river. It was a disorderly mob and it grew until the roadway was almost full.

Perc came over and jerked his head toward the crowd. "We decided to call a vote here and now, Cleve; me and Eric and the rest of the committee."

"What kind of a vote, Perc?"

"To see if the men want their mayor to represent them before the Legislature."

Cleve shifted his weight, looking past the sheriff at the sea of dirty faces.

Stevens nodded at Perc. "That's a good idea; the sooner Gold River acts, the better. You're going to take a vocal vote, I reckon?"

Perc nodded, and turned back to the miners without answering. His voice rose and grew squeaky until the bedlam died, then he stated the issues succinctly and paused for the vote, holding his thin arm in the air.

The response was immediate — and deafening. Perc made a wry face at the newcomers, who blinked at the thunderous roar, then he turned back and called for differences. There were none. The road was as quiet as it had been noisy moments before.

The sheriff's leathery face wreathed into a seamed smile. "There's your answer, boys; Cleve, what are you standing there for?"

Commissioner Stevens laughed heartily and looked at Cleve. "All right, boys; there's your answer. When does the next stage pull out?"

Cleve fished out his pocket watch and studied it soberly, still a little confused and bewildered by the complete faith the miners had in the committee — and especially in himself. "Not for about two hours, Commissioner." He offered a thin smile. "If it's on time, I mean."

Marshal Hendricks ran a thin hand along his jaw, appraising Cleve's clothing with a wry look. "I reckon that'll be about as long as you'll need to scrape that dirt off you." He looked up with an ironic smile. "And the beard, too — unless you're figuring on letting it grow out."

Cleve looked uncertainly at Perc. "Well, all right; Perc, will you take these gentlemen over while I get spruced up a little?"

Perc nodded his agreement and wagged his head back and forth in mock commiseration at Cleve's unkempt appearance. "Darned if

I know whether a man can scrape forty-eight hours of grime off in two or three hours, or not."

The men who heard him laughed as Cleve edged through the milling miners and headed for his shack. He was abreast of Cathy's café, seeing the men coming and going through the battered door, when he had an inspiration and turned in.

The girl was shiny-nosed and busy, but she saw Cleve instantly and stopped in mid-stride to look into his face, her eyes searching anxiously. He smiled, and the relief was instantly apparent in the way she relaxed.

"Cathy, come here a minute, will you?"

She came. They were clear of the men, who winked owlishly at one another. He lowered his voice. "I'm going to the Territorial capital to talk before the Legislature. Will you come with me?"

She nodded with scarcely a moment's hesitation. "Yes; when?"

"On the next stage; there's a United States Marshal and a Territorial Commissioner going along, too. I'll go —"

"Cleve, is there any trouble?"

"No, Cathy; I'll explain later. Right now I've got to get cleaned up. I'll come back by here and get you."

"All right." She wiped her hands unconsciously on her apron as she watched Cleve go up the street and disappear among the miners who swarmed the plankwalk.

There was the same uneasiness in her, but it was laced with pride in her man now, too.

CHAPTER SIX

Territorial Legislature

Cleve Simpson, freshly bathed, shaved and rested after the long stage ride, during which he slept almost constantly between relays, arrived in the bustling capital with Cathy on his arm and both Stevens and Hendricks smiling encouragement.

The sky was cloudy and held a threat of storm, but Cathy didn't notice. She had never seen a town larger than Gold River before, unless it was a rare trip to Jacksonville. The huge dray wagons with their handsome teams, as much as the flashy gigs and sedate, fringe-topped runabouts and buggies, fascinated her.

She clung to Cleve's arm as the men sought out an hotel, registered Cathy and Cleve in adjoining rooms, then freshened up and went to the Territorial Administration building to present Cleve Simpson, mayor of Gold River. A request to address the Legislature, which was in session, was drafted and submitted through the gnarled old clerk; then Cathy and

Cleve were left alone. The Commissioner excused himself on the ground that he personally wanted to press Cleve's petition in order that the man from Gold River might be heard the following day; the United States Marshal had his own fences to mend, also. They parted with an agreement to meet at Cleve's rooms the following morning and have breakfast together at the hotel.

Out in the busy street again, caught up in a swirl of well-dressed pedestrians, Cathy and Cleve went arm-in-arm on a sightseeing tour through Oregon City. The girl was thrilled and buoyant, laughing up into Cleve's face and enjoying every minute of their day.

Then, after supper, when the storm clouds had crystallised into large drops of rain that fell softly in the night, they stood on the hotel porch, watching the night close over the land. There was a smell of freshness, of washed air, in the darkness.

Cleve looked down at the erect figure of the girl beside him. In her very best outfit, Cathy was beautiful. The night, too, had a magic hand in the moment of enchantment. "Let's be married while we're here, Cathy."

She looked up at him. "Tonight?"

"Well, I'm afraid it's too late for that. In the morning, before we go to the Legislature, maybe we could find a minister who'd —"

"No; not tomorrow, Cleve. Tonight — right now!"

Cleve felt the blood rise behind his face. It was a wonderful night and they were on the verge of Gold River's triumph; both felt it — and they were in love. He shifted his weight, raised his eyes from her eager, flushed face, and looked into the steady drizzle.

"All right," he said. "You wait here; I'll see if I can find a minister who'll —"

"I'll come with you." She turned away and didn't see his surprised look. "There's a cab over there by that overhang. Come on."

She was pulling at his arm. Cleve gave way before her insistence, and together they went through the drizzle and jumped into the cab. The driver shot them a startled look, then opened the little square hole in the top of the rig and peered wonderingly in at them.

Cleve smiled up, dabbing at the moisture on his face. "Do you know where there's a minister, pardner?"

The man regarded him with a dawning light. "Marryin' or buryin', mister?"

Cathy's eyes were sparkling with excitement. "Marrying."

"Yes'm; there's several. The priest is down —"

"Take us to the nearest one, friend," Cleve said. "The quicker the better."

The minister, a handsome, portly man with a great shock of white hair, squinted at his breathless visitors and seemed to catch some of their verve. He waved them into a parlour complete with antimacassars and the odour of mothballs, then excused himself.

Cathy was studying Cleve with small doubts and acute embarrassment. "Cleve; do you think — I mean, I was awfully — forward, wasn't I? Maybe you'd rather think a little. I mean, wouldn't you —"

Cleve laughed and reached for her, wagging his head a little. "You're a darned paradox, Cathy; first you hesitated, then you despised me — and now you're marrying me. By God, Cathy, I think there's fire in you."

He was still holding her, feeling the excitement of her nearness, when the minister came back into the parlour dressed in a staid black coat, his hair combed loosely, and a pair of handsome turtle-rimmed spectacles perched over his forehead.

"I believe that the custom normally is to wait for an appointment for this service, friends." There was an amused irony in his words.

Cleve smiled and apologised, feeling embarrassed at what he considered the clergyman might be thinking. "You have objections, then? Perhaps we'd better come —"

"No," the man answered in a slow drawl, a broad smile creasing his face. "But your selection of ministers was fortunate. Generally speaking, my colleagues don't favour these spur-of-the-moment unions."

Cathy was crimson and uncomfortable. She looked from Cleve to the minister, saying nothing.

Cleve read the subdued good nature in the preacher's face and nodded. "We are required to have a witness, are we not?"

"Yes; my wife's coming down as soon as she gets dressed. So while we're waiting, if you'll give me your names and so on. . . ."

The service was simple and thrilling to both Cathy and Cleve. They left the house and kissed in the rain, under the frankly interested stare of the waiting hackman, who thought them slightly insane, or at least uninhibited and bordering on neurotic precociousness.

At the hotel, they each drank a glass of champagne in silent and secret celebration of their marriage, then went upstairs. Cathy's eyes were wide with doubt, and something akin to fright and eagerness, when Cleve took her to his quarters.

Both smiled bashfully as Cleve put Cathy down in the middle of the floor; he watched her standing in the centre of the room, looking at him without expression, and laughed softly.

She lowered her eyes, and Cleve tilted her head back with his hand. "Darling, you're a wife now. Those funny little inhibitions of yours will be laid to rest."

"It will be a new life for both of us, Cleve."

He heard the timidity in her voice, and gathered her up close and kissed her tenderly. The rain fell softly, constantly, against the hotel roof. It made a soothing sound that didn't abate until the following morning, when they went downstairs to breakfast. There they met Stevens, who assured them that Cleve's petition had been accepted and he was to address the Legislature at ten o'clock sharp.

Cathy received the Commissioner's smiling congratulations in confusion, but by the time the U.S. Marshal joined them at the table, she had recovered her decorum sufficiently to acknowledge the good wishes for her husband and herself with a minimum of high colouring.

Just outside the staid chambers of the Territorial Legislature, Stevens touched Cleve's arm. "One thing to remember, Mister Simpson: these men are concerned primarily with the welfare of Oregon. They're men like you and me, and Hendricks, here. They want the same things for the Territory that you do; order and decency and, eventually, statehood. Say exactly what you think — in your own words. Be abrupt, if you feel you must, but be comprehensive. Give them the full story. I'll be in my place, ready to back you up any time you need me." Stevens turned to Hendricks. "Marshal, will you escort Mrs. Simpson to the gallery?"

The Federal lawman smiled at Cathy and bowed slightly from the waist. "That's a pleasure that exceeds the honour of hearing her husband address the Legislature."

Cathy's eyes sparkled. She returned the bow with a half-humorous, half-mocking curtsy, saying nothing. Then she reached out, took Cleve's hand, and held it tightly, looking into his face for a brief second, breathing a wife's prayer for the success of her husband. Then she left on Hendricks's arm for the spectators' gallery entrance.

The room was large and draughty. Cleve saw the rows of eyes turn at his entry. He listened stiffly as Commissioner Stevens introduced him. Then he was alone in the silence, feeling the gravity of the situation — yet almost afraid to start speaking. His eyes roamed the faces that were looking at him. Here was the peak of his efforts; all that had gone before — even Sam Lamarr's death — had been but the foundation upon which Cleve Simpson would build Gold River. Cleve was acutely aware of his mission, and he allowed his eyes to wander up to the gallery as he assimilated his thoughts. Cathy was somewhere up there; he could not distinguish one out of a host of indistinguishable faces, yet he felt that it was there, and from the knowledge he drew his strength.

As if by a magnet, his glance was drawn to one face in the gallery. Cathy nodded reassuringly down at him, and his lips turned up just a little at the corners.

When he spoke, there was humility in his voice; mingled with it was respect and an awesome realisation of why he was standing in front of so august a body as the Legislature. It sobered him to think that a miner with dirty hands and not too much education could be heard.

"Gentlemen; I'm speaking to you as the mayor of Gold River, the spokesman appointed by the miners — and as a man who wants order where chaos now exists." He told them of Willis's plans for the assay office and mint. Carefully, he carried them from the first violence that had culminated in Sam Lamarr's death right up to the present. He spoke of the nightly violence, the murders, the robberies and the lawlessness that had prevailed in Gold River. He told them of his trip to Jacksonville, and how he had lain flat behind a dead horse in the middle of the road to escape assassins' bullets. He touched briefly on Ben

Carter's lynching, and humility was evident in his voice as he laid the blame at the feet of the very men who had sent him to the Legislature.

He finished his honest, frank interpretation of the mess that was Gold River in its brawling youth with the blowing up of the Gold River House and the arrival of Commissioner Stevens and United States Marshal Hendricks.

Cleve's voice reverberated through the draughty hall now; gone was the timidity of doubt, replaced by the firm clarity of deep conviction. There was a tense silence when Cleve finally finished, and he stood awaiting questions from the men before him. He allowed a brief glance at his wife, whose face was pale and stiff. But the light in her eyes was his reward; it shone with pride and sympathy — and love.

"Mister Simpson." Cleve looked down at the man. He was tall, aged and bent. "Before the meeting, we discussed this situation with Commissioner Stevens. He informed us of the ruthlessness of this man Willis. Now then, young man; we appreciate your generosity towards your foe, which you have been careful not to paint in anything but a competitive light, but we want to know more about this man."

The Speaker turned slowly and picked up

a paper from the table in front of him. "You see, we have a petition here, presented yesterday, calling for the Territorial militia to enforce the law in Gold River and Jacksonville sufficiently to allow Willis to erect his mint and assay office as authorised by the Federal government."

Cleve was dumbfounded. Willis, after eluding the posses around Gold River, had actually had the gall to ride straight to Oregon City and try to force his will on the people of Gold River by the use of troops. That meant but one thing to Cleve: Harold and Neila Willis were in the capital!

The tall, elderly Speaker was staring at him intently. "Well?" he said dryly.

"Gentlemen," Cleve began again. "This is disturbing news to me. There is little I can say about it beyond this: Willis is wanted in Gold River for complicity in the murder of Sheriff Sam Lamarr. He is also wanted for suspicion of abetting robbery, murder and pillage. If you gentlemen feel inclined to consider the petition of a man on whom the stigma of murder — or, at least, suspicion of murder — lies, then I can't influence you in any way."

The Speaker nodded, rubbing his chin with a bony hand. "But, Mister Simpson, is there any proof of these claims? You must realise that the Legislature is being asked to choose between your faction and that of Harold Willis. We know neither of you well enough to decide without proof of the charges that you both have made." A brief, pregnant pause preceded the crusher. "What we must have is actual proof of Willis's complicity in the murder of this man Lamarr, and of the other charges you have brought against Willis. Suffice it to say that, without proof, we will be unable to honour your claim over Willis's petition."

Cleve shook his head. "I'm afraid, sir, that we have no proof. All we do have is the knowledge — and this goes for every man in Gold River — that Harold Willis is behind the ruthlessness that struck when the miners decided to clean up Gold River."

Cathy's voice came clearly from the gallery. Cleve turned at the sound of her voice, as did the legislators, in surprise and wonder. He saw his wife standing beside the Federal Marshal, her blue eyes flashing with indignation, her bosom heaving with the passion of her conviction in Cleve's right, and he was held spellbound.

Aroused as he knew she could be, Cathy was as eloquent, savage and fiery as Cleve knew any woman would be. "Gentlemen, I'll give you proof."

For several seconds, silence reigned. Then,

sensing no one would intervene, Cathy spoke. "Mister Simpson is my husband; but he has been in the saddle and on the committee meetings so much lately that he only knows one side of this battle.

"I have a café in Gold River; I hear a lot of things there, and until now I've considered the things I've heard as confidences that were not to be repeated, because the men who said them were careless in my presence. Well, I'll tell you two instances of the things I've heard, and you can judge Harold Willis by them."

The tall, gaunt Speaker looked enquiringly at the Master-at-arms. That keeper of order in the Legislature was being restrained from interfering with the impromptu speaker by three scowling legislators who told him bluntly to let her finish. The Master-at-arms looked helplessly at the Speaker and shrugged his shoulders. The elderly man smiled a little and also shrugged, then resumed his seat.

Cleve was rigid, fearing that Cathy's outburst might ruin the chances of Gold River's success, but a glance at Commissioner Stevens told him that this was not the case — so far. His wife's voice went on clearly, musically and decisively, dropping words like bullets in the silence of the vast room.

"Mister Willis hired a man named Thorpe to come to Gold River and open a private assayer's office. Thorpe and Ben Carter discussed it in my café. Thorpe said he thought the reason was because of the opportunities to rob miners on the roads between the two towns, and also that Willis had bribed Owen Byrd, the government supervisor of the assay office in Jacksonville, to water the gold content of the coins be made for the miners by adding a liberal amount of foreign metals to the mixture. In many cases they planned to reduce the actual gold content by as much as one-half.

"I took it upon myself to warn the residents of Jacksonville of these things by sending an anonymous letter over there to the effect that Willis and Byrd were planning to rob the miners."

There was a low buzz in the room that subsided only when the Speaker banged his gavel. Cleve was smiling; he remembered the letter posted up in the saloon in Jacksonville.

Cathy went on. "I can give you my word, gentlemen, that I heard these things." She looked at Cleve. "But, like my husband, I can't prove them."

Another buzz of opinion floated on the tense air. The Speaker nodded at Cathy. "Did you ever hear anything said that would lead you to believe that Willis was implicated in either the attack on your husband over in Jacksonville, or in the death of this man Lamarr, madam?"

Cathy shook her head. She was feeling both defeat and bitterness. A hand touched her wrist lightly. She turned to see the Federal Marshal rise and stand beside her.

Marshal Hendricks bowed slightly at the upturned faces. "If I may interrupt briefly, gentlemen; I have proof that Harold Willis bribed a Federal assayer, planned the attempted murder of Cleve Simpson, here, and engineered this entire lawlessness from start to finish."

There was a second of intense silence, then a sound of low voices broke over the room until the Speaker struck testily with his gavel again and reminded the legislators that silence was not only the custom, but the rule as well. Gradually the noise subsided, but the looks of surprise and eagerness persisted.

The Speaker was looking directly at Hendricks when he spoke. "Mister Hendricks, you are a United States Marshal, are you not, sir?"

"Yes, sir; stationed at San Francisco."

"Yes. Well, would you explain to us — for the record — exactly what your concern is in this affair?"

"Certainly. I was ordered here when news of the killings at Gold River came into our office from several sources. My first duty was to contact your Commissioner Stevens for permission to exercise Federal authority in conjunction with your people, in the Territory, in re-establishing and maintaining law and order at Gold River."

"And?"

"The Commissioner and myself went to Gold River, conducted an investigation, found the affair to be as represented here today, and requested Mister Simpson to come back with us to present his case before you," Hendricks said.

The Speaker eyed Hendricks speculatively. "You said you have proof; I'd like to remind you, sir, that proof — above all else — will determine the stand this Legislature will take in this affair. We have two men, neither of whom is known to us, who accuse each other of illegal acts. In order for us to arrive at any conclusion at all, we must have proof of cupidity. Mister Hendricks, does your proof bear directly on this situation in such a manner that the Territorial Legislature can use it in arriving at a just decision?"

"Yes, sir; it does."

"Specifically, what is the nature of this proof?"

"The Federal assayer in Jacksonville, Owen Byrd, is in the custody of the sheriff of Gold River. During my stay at Gold River, I interviewed Mister Byrd. He readily told me all he knew about Harold Willis, and on the strength of his confession I sent a letter off by special courier to my office in San Francisco yesterday afternoon, requesting that immediate steps be taken to furnish me with a warrant for Willis's arrest on the specifications presented this morning by Mister Simpson." Hendricks paused, looked at the faces turned up to him, and went on in a low, even voice. "If it is the purpose of the Legislature to consider the petition of Harold Willis for the establishment of his Federally-approved mint at Jacksonville, then I'd like to point out that not only are you considering the petition of a fugitive from justice, but you are also considering the petition of a man who will be discredited as soon as my reports reach Washington; I sent a duplicate request there for permission to arrest Willis, and also asked for immediate revocation of approval granted him for the mint and assay office."

Cleve was in the best position to see the reaction to Hendricks's curt speech. First, the legislation remained in a state of silent shock; then, gradually, they turned to one another, talking in low voices. The sound swelled, rolling in a deep crescendo that ignored the sharp banging of the Speaker's gavel until the tall, bent old man stood to his full height, face tight in outrage, and shouted stentoriously into the teeth of the bedlam until it was hushed enough for him to speak.

The words were biting, angry and blunt. "Gentlemen; because of the astonishing intelligence from the delegation from Gold River," he paused here to bow gallantly towards Cathy, who was sitting, white-faced, beside Hendricks, and to include Cleve in the gesture, before he continued, "I think there's really little choice left to us."

Before the murmur could get out of hand again, he went on, lowering his voice so that the listeners would have to remain quiet in order to hear him. "There is a factor here that concerns us, and not the delegation from Gold River. We want statehood!"

Spontaneous cries erupted briefly. "This condition at Gold River puts us squarely in the position of antagonising the Federal government, should we back Willis's petition. Not only that, but, as Mister Hendricks pointed out, we would be fostering a man who, while not yet a criminal, will be shortly."

The shock of white hair lowered slightly and the hard old eyes flashed over the room. "There is no choice, either ethically, morally or constitutionally; I am asking for your immediate approval of a legislative plan — and backing — to establish a mint temporarily,

153

under Territorial jurisdiction, at Gold River, to be directed by Mister Cleve Simpson, subject to his acceptance of the post and your disapproval of the petition made by Harold Willis."

Again the Speaker paused, looked out over the room, and smiled softly. "And I am further asking that we take a hand vote — here and now — in this motion."

Cleve saw the Speaker's motion seconded, then the vote was taken. It was not only unanimous, but the recording of that vote was noisily and enthusiastically received.

The Speaker again called for silence, turned to Cleve, and nodded his head. "Mister Simpson, can the Territory of Oregon call on you as a man who has steadfastly fought for the kind of thing we need in order to achieve our goal of statehood, to serve in the capacity of director of a branch mint to be established at Gold River? And further, because of the dire need for acceptable coinage, can we depend upon you to take charge of this mint temporarily until such time that the United States government can and will take over?"

Cleve darted a quick look at Cathy. She was nodding her head vigorously at him. He fought down a smile, then spoke. "Mister Speaker; I'm honoured by the offer and accept with the promise that I will do my best to serve

the miners and the Territory of Oregon —
although I'm not sure that I'm fitted for such
a position, being a gold miner by trade, not
a politician, sir."

There were some snickers in the audience
that made Cleve redden. The Speaker smiled
at Cleve before he answered. His voice was
dryly humorous. "Well, Mister Simpson, I
venture the belief that not a man-jack among
us today hasn't had to scrape river mud from
under his fingernails at some time since coming to the Territory. Also, I am fairly confident
that the same constituent who backed you
so heartily a few moments back will be more
than happy to oversee you in this new trust,
too." He bowed again, humorously, towards
Cathy.

She smiled with a mist of tears in her eyes,
and the legislators let out a roar of laughter,
shot through with words of encouragement
and approval.

Cleve looked up at Cathy, caught her glance,
and held it firmly for several seconds. She
dabbed at the tears at the corners of her eyes,
and he smiled up at her reassuringly. It was
almost with reluctance that Cleve lowered his
glance to the Speaker, nodded in appreciation for what he had done, and, after shaking hands with him, moved slowly out of
the hall.

Even as he went, Cleve's eyes roamed the gallery for a sight of Cathy. It was evident from the clearness of his eyes and the firm reassurance of his step that much had been accomplished.

CHAPTER SEVEN

End of Empire

Cleve Simpson was standing a little apart from Cathy, who was talking to the Commissioner, when he saw someone coming towards him through the group of people standing in the outer chamber of the Legislature.

His attention was diverted, however, by Marshal Hendricks. "Mister Simpson, I'm eternally grateful that you miners didn't get your hands on Owen Byrd."

Cleve nodded fervently. "Amen to that," he said with a grin. "If it hadn't been for him, I'm afraid things wouldn't have come out so well. Byrd and you. I meant to say. That talk you gave was wonderful, Marshal."

Hendricks smiled wryly. "Well, I really had no business butting in like that, but —"

"Cleve! Oh, darling!"

Cleve was jerked wildly half-around, sideways to the equally astonished Marshal, and found himself looking down into the ebony-black eyes of Neila Willis. He was dumbfounded. Neila threw her arms around his

157

neck, clinging to him with a shamelessness that made the people in the outer chamber stare at both of them.

He had no chance to glimpse Cathy before Neila's voice was recklessly, imploringly begging him to forgive her for what she had said and done at Jacksonville. "Oh, darling; I was crazy with anger — with jealousy. I prayed that you'd survive — and you did."

Her beautiful face was working in a frenzy; the hands were clutching him so wildly that the pain gyrated outwards from the bruised flesh under her hands. "Cleve, Cleve! I didn't mean what I said at all. I do want you — more than ever. I left Harold when I heard that you were here. I told him why, too — because I love you, Cleve. I love you!"

It all happened so fast, with such startling speed, that no one had moved; they were still staring, beginning to come out of the trance of shock that held them, when the room rocked to a blasting explosion.

Several voices erupted in squeals of terror. Neila convulsed against Cleve, gazing up into his face with a look of incredible stupor and bewilderment. Then she fell away from him limply, looking to Cleve at that moment like a broken doll, and collapsed at his feet with her arms flung outwards as if to ward off the jarring impact of the floor.

The screeching of frightened people seemed to stop, as if they had found something to divert their eyes and ears, and they stood cringing, searching, trying to find safety and at the same time not daring to miss any of the drama that was being unfolded before their eyes. In the brief moment that Cleve took to sweep the room with his glance, he saw the shocked spectators, eyes wide in fear, many biting the knuckles of their hands until they showed pasty-white.

In the midst of the confusion, Hendricks knelt swiftly and rolled the woman over and stared at her in disbelief. Cleve watched, spellbound and unmoving; he saw the slight trickle of scarlet that had stopped almost before it began to flow from under her left arm, halfway down her side.

Awakened now, Cleve mentally calculated the course of the bullet, and he stood unsteadily, knowing that Neila Willis was dead — her heart punctured by the shot that had climaxed her assault upon him. He was raising his eyes towards Cathy when the second shot rang out, reverberating through the hollow chamber. Cleve flinched at the searing pain that burned almost unbearably across his stomach; he turned towards the sound, seeing nothing but badly frightened people scattering like wild birds in a wind.

Thoroughly awakened now, and equally aroused, Cleve pulled the .44 from his pocket and ran towards the doors that opened on to the still-wet roadway. People were erupting from the legislative building like quail, seldom looking back, eager to put distance between themselves and the men who fired guns so freely — and accurately.

Cleve stood still, searching the whiplash of movement. Then he saw what he was looking for, raised his gun deliberately, aimed, and cursed ragingly when two women darted between him and the fleeing Harold Willis. Angrily, Cleve lowered his gun, and went after his assailant.

The day was grey with swollen clouds, and the roadways were slippery paths of bone-hard earth with little pools of murky, dirty water in them. Cleve's mood matched the dismal scenes he raced through, feeling the soreness in his abdomen, cold and unfriendly.

At that moment, Cleve wondered why he was racing after Harold Willis. He — the advocate of justice — was running after a man who had seen fit to break the laws at will, unmindful of the consequences beyond his own gain. There was a gun in his hand, and he had already tried to rob justice by usurping its rights to weigh Willis's guilt. Cleve's mood was many things; most of all, it was one of anger that such a man as Willis could put himself above the law.

Cleve got off one shot as the panicked Willis turned and stood fast long enough to fire twice more, then the wild-eyed man flung the pepperbox Derringer from him and raced away. Cleve had that one still moment to fire.

He saw Willis rock back a little, but the fugitive's unimpaired gait as he ran for his life didn't indicate that he was hard hit.

As Cleve saw Willis move swiftly away, he imagined that he was watching a mad dog flee for his very life; it was no longer a matter of right or wrong. A mad dog should be exterminated, and the job fell to whomever the dog had bitten. Cleve's eyes dropped to his own stomach, and he knew then that the mad dog had bitten his last man.

Cleve was tiring fast by the time he saw the man leap wildly into a rig tied before an apothecary's shop, slash at the startled buggy-horse with the whip, and career madly through the amazed traffic. One glimpse of the drawn, white face as the man looked back told Cleve that his prey was escaping.

Bitterness raged through him — bitterness and blind fury. Without a second thought, Cleve swerved off the sidewalk, raced to a nearby hitchrail, made a rapid selection and untied the horse in a flurry of reins. He flung himself aboard and spun out into the traffic, heeling the startled animal into a belly-down run that split the pedestrians and wheeled traffic like a flashing knife-blade.

Shouts arose in the angry wake behind them; men stood erect in red-faced rage from their wagon and buggy seats, flourishing fists at the racing buggy and its equally wildly riding pursuit.

The traffic thinned. Cleve was gaining a little, but Willis had a good head start, and the horse that drew his rig was bred for fine-harness speed. The buildings flashed by in a blur, until they were farther apart, then infrequent. Finally, the open stretches lay ahead, with ranches straddling the road that led in an undulating, unbroken straight line as far as the eye could see.

Cleve fired three times in rapid succession; only once did he see the long splinter of wood fly out of the buggy. Cursing, he flung the empty gun from him and pressed his hand over the sodden, scarlet stickiness that was his lower shirt-front. The soreness was increasing, and Cleve gritted his teeth at the throbbing pain that was weakening him with the slow, measured persistence of a leech.

A rambling, old, unpainted ranch-house loomed ahead, set back from the road with a ruggedly austere look. Harold Willis turned the buggy with a recklessness that made it slide two-wheeled into the dirt lane. It weaved uncertainly, straightened out, and Cleve watched it whip towards the old house.

Willis left the rig in a flying bound that carried him half-way to the house. Then he was through the front door and lost from sight.

Cleve came off the sweating horse a little stiffly, awkwardly, and ran towards the building. The grinding ache in his stomach was a throbbing reminder that haste was imperative. He threw caution to the winds as he kicked the door open, stood hesitantly framed in the opening, then he stepped into the vacant, musty-smelling room and kicked the panel closed behind him with a booted foot.

The old house was stale with the smell and atmosphere of all deserted buildings. Cleve saw the stairway in the gloominess of the house. His eyes dropped to the floor, and he traced out the faint impressions there in the gathered dust of recently made boot-prints. He went forward slowly, his eyes piercing the cloying darkness for something with which to arm himself. There was nothing — just a three-legged table with the fourth leg lying in the accumulated refuse piled haphazardly near one corner of the room.

Cleve grabbed up the table leg, hefted its oaken stubbiness in his reddened hands, felt the soundness of the bludgeon, and turned again towards the stairs.

From up above, Cleve could hear a sound like the scurrying of rats. "Willis, come down out of there!"

There was no answer.

Cleve's face was savage. He went to the bottom of the stairs, glanced up, tested the dusty railing with his free hand, and began a slow, wary advance up the rickety steps towards the second floor.

Each footstep made the old wood protest in creaking, reverberating sounds that seemed to swell through the silent house. Cleve cursed to himself. Willis could hear the noise, and he could tell by the sound exactly where Cleve was each time he moved. Cleve shrugged philosophically; as long as they were both unarmed, no one had any clear-cut advantage.

Cleve felt equal, despite the pain of his wound, and he had an inner feeling that nothing on earth — including the man who waited upstairs for him — would keep him from exacting the penalty. For his crimes against them all, back in Gold River, and here in Oregon City as well, Harold Willis would pay a stiff price. There could be no other way for either of them. Each, in his own way, felt that right — or reason — was his ally, and both knew that one man might walk out of this house, but not both.

Cleve was half-way up the old stairway when the quick sound of boots, urgently, frantically moving overhead, made him glance up. Willis stood above him, balancing, the muscles in his rigid neck bunched under the great weight of a battered old oaken dresser.

Cleve saw his danger and paused for the space of a single second, until Willis leaned forward, easing off the great weight and letting it drop. Then he took four steps in two large movements forward, upward, and the massive cabinet crashed behind him with a ripping, tearing sound that shook the entire old shell of the house, sending echoes hollowly reverberating through its frame again and again.

Instinctively, Cleve glanced back, and saw the stairs behind him broken for the space of nearly five feet. Cleve lunged for the upper landing, made it, and turned towards the open door through which Willis had just disappeared.

Cleve halted just outside the room, hefted his table leg again, and peered into the gloomy, grey interior where the dismal day lent no shadow or light.

"Willis." He paused for a breath. "Come out of there!"

The only answer was the sinister stillness

that held the house in its grip since their entrance.

"Willis — if you come out, I'll take you back a prisoner. If you don't come out, I'll come in there and drag you out!"

Surprised, Cleve got his answer. "Come ahead; step through the damned door, Simpson. Try it."

Cleve was beyond reason. Only one thing motivated him: the apprehension of Harold Willis — alive or dead — and soon. The throbbing in his stomach, growing as the minutes ticked by, would soon overwhelm him. Cleve's face showed determination to stay on his feet until he had subdued Willis, who now had become a symbol for all the deaths and suffering in Cleve Simpson's life — all the evil and treachery.

Cleve gripped his club, rocked forward a little, and leaped into the grey maw that was the doorway. Something flashed at him, grazing his shoulders and tearing the cloth of his coat down the back. Then he was whirling, staring at the man he wanted to kill.

Willis was ashen-faced, flattened against the musty old wall. His eyes were bulging with the insane, desperate look of a cornered rat, and the courage of a cornered rat was shining out at Cleve. Willis held a nine-inch-bladed boot-knife in his hand, low.

166

Cleve felt the flesh along his back crawl. Willis's slash at his back had been close. The dullness of the long blade was lightest up along the cutting edge. Cleve gripped the old table leg tighter in his big fist and stepped lightly forward, so that Willis's path to the door was cut off. If Willis were to leave that room alive, Cleve knew it would have to be over his own body.

"Drop it!"

Willis said nothing; he just shook his head. His body was tensed and ready, like a coiled spring.

"Willis, you're a fool." There was vast contempt in Cleve's voice. There was weariness in it, too. "That knife's no weapon against this." He flexed his arm, and watched Willis's eyes travel the length and width of the club in his hand. "You've lost out all round; keep on fighting, and you'll lose the only thing you've got left — your life."

Willis's eyes were held on the club, as if it fascinated him. His trapped courage came up slowly, as the natural fear of a pursued animal vanished before the tangible, possibly fallible, foe before him. He shook his head with a rabid, mad-dog look on his face. "Yeah, Simpson; I've got one thing left. By God, I'll keep it, too. You've got everything else, damn your soul — even Neila." His eyes clouded

167

over at the mention of her name. "Well —"

"I never wanted her."

Willis jerked his head violently in anger. "No, maybe not. But that doesn't change a thing. Maybe it makes it even worse. If you steal a man's wife on purpose, at least he's lost something worth stealing. But when you went after her, damn you, you did it without wanting her, and you left me nothing. Nothing at all." Willis was beyond reason now. The words jumbled out of his mouth and his eyes shone eerily in the gloom of the room. "You didn't want her and I did, but she turned on me. That's something a man can't justify to himself. He's got something he can't have, and something no one else wants, either."

Cleve shook his head, eyes boring into Willis's. "I don't follow you, but it doesn't make any difference. Just one thing matters now: you're responsible for Sam Lamarr's death — and Neila's, too. Indirectly, you've been the cause of other deaths and a lot of suffering. You've had your fling, Willis; now drop that knife and walk out of the room ahead of me — slowly."

Willis's thin lips spread back, parted and flat against his teeth. "Like hell," he said softly. "Like hell I will; I wouldn't last fifteen minutes in Gold River, Simpson — and you know it. That's why you want to make me

168

go back there. No — I won't go back."

Cleve shrugged. "I don't know; maybe the trial would be here, in Oregon City." He spread his hands in a gesture that spoke volumes to Willis. "Anyway, you've got it coming. You should —"

Willis laughed harshly. "Maybe, but you sure won't be around to see it."

Cleve studied the shorter, burly man for a silent moment, and saw that all reason had deserted him. His offer of life had been refused, and Cleve knew that he would have to kill the man before him, if he didn't know before. He pursed his lips and started forward.

Willis swore monotonously at him, moving away, his wide eyes watching Cleve's face for the tell-tale tightening that would be a signal of the younger man's intention of attack. He was disappointed. Cleve showed no emotion at all, just a steady, shuffling sort of movement that managed to keep the doorway blocked to Willis.

Then Cleve lunged like lightning, still deceiving Willis by his blankness of facial expression, and lashed out with the club. Willis saw the blow coming; Cleve couldn't raise and strike out with the club without giving ample warning to Willis. Both men realized that the club was not a weapon designed for lightning attacks. Both men realized that the knife in

Willis's hand was.

The descending bludgeon tore into empty space as Willis jumped swiftly away. Cleve went forward, drawn off balance by momentum. Willis turned back and slashed, but he, too, couldn't halt his impetus enough to strike damagingly at Cleve.

Backing away, still keeping the door barred to Willis, Cleve stalked him, watching the knife. Willis feinted and Cleve just shook his head, refusing to be sucked into the trap, and then the saloon owner threw caution to the winds. He tore in at Cleve with the knife searing the grey atmosphere like a living shaft of steel.

Cleve gave way several steps, brought the club recklessly off to one side, high, and left himself open to Willis's blade. The crazed Willis lunged in. The club whistled.

Too late, Harold Willis knew that he had been feinted into a trap. The club didn't have far to travel. It came downward and slightly inward. The jolt carried all the way up Cleve's arm, into the writhing shoulder muscles, and part way down his back, when it struck Willis's head. It had the effect on Cleve of running into a stone wall.

Cleve heard the knife clatter to the floor, and he stepped away, watching in fascination as Willis bent inward from the belt as though his legs still refused to admit defeat. Willis hung awkwardly in that position for a second, then broke over and crumpled. Cleve looked down at him, seeing the strange flatness of his body.

He deliberately bent, scooped up the knife and walked out of the room, found a window and tossed the blade out into the sulky drizzle that was beginning to fall from the leaden skies overhead. He glanced down, saw the droopy-headed horse he had ridden to the final rendezvous, standing beside the top-buggy that had been Willis's transportation.

Cleve started to turn back. Something caught his attention, and he turned tiredly back to the window. A body of horsemen, about six or seven in number, were riding, hunched over against the drizzle, down the road from the direction of Oregon City.

He watched them turn in at the abandoned ranch-house entry lane and come towards him in a sloppy, mud-larking gallop. Cleve recognised only one man, United States Marshal Hendricks, leading the riders.

He went back into the room where Harold Willis lay, sat on the edge of the warped, broken wall-bed that seemed to hang in the air, and dropped his club.

There was the ache, dull now and no longer angry, in the pit of his stomach. Cleve methodically pulled at the stiff shirting, opened it, and dabbed at the thick welter of drying blood on his flesh. The examination was cursory and he didn't find the wound until his finger located the swollen hole. Then Cleve traced the path of the tiny slug with a sense of relief and silent gratitude. He recalled now that he had been standing sideways to Willis — as had Neila — when the slug had struck him. It had entered his stomach just under the skin, and had ridden in a flat trajectory between the stomach muscles and the flesh itself, until the curve of his body had forced it back out of the flesh about ten inches from the point of entry.

Cleve felt gingerly. The route the bullet had travelled was ridged in swollen, sore flesh, like the welt of a whiplash, but it lay just below the skin. The loss of blood hadn't been slight, but in his relief he attributed to this a secondary importance.

He was still sitting there, feeling comfortably drowsy and relaxed, when the rush of boots stormed into the house and hurried to the stairway. The ruin of the shattered stairs presented a profane obstacle for a moment. Then, men were crowding into the room, strangers staring at him in amazement, until Hendricks pushed through them with a set, angry look around his eyes.

Cleve nodded. "Gentlemen?" he said.

Hendricks moved in close, bent without a word, and studied the wound in Cleve's stomach. He probed it gently, his eyes wide as he recognised how lucky the path of the bullet had been to Cleve, He straightened, the hard glint still in his eyes. "Boy, that was some chase. Oregon City's up in arms. The Commissioner's taking care of it, though. Tell me, Cleve, how do you feel?"

Cleve smiled wanly. "A little tired."

Hendricks was looking at him closely. "I would imagine so," he said dryly. "You've lost quite a bit of blood." The Marshal turned, motioned the possemen to move away from where they had clustered around Willis, and he bent to examine him.

The examination was brief and callous. When he rose, his eyes roved over the silent, watching men who stood by in awkward groups.

"Three, four of you boys take him downstairs." Hendricks jerked his thumb.

One of the men, a swarthy man with an oily, ferocious-looking beard and moustache, nodded, then looked over at Willis. "Lash him across a horse?"

Cleve looked up quickly, saw Hendricks nod his head, and watched as the men hoisted the limp body gingerly and with evident distaste

173

for their job, and move towards the doorway, shove through it, and disappear.

Hendricks came back to where Cleve still sat on the bed, and leaned against the wall. He made a cigarette, lighted it and handed it to Cleve, who accepted it silently and inhaled long and deeply.

"Dead?"

Hendricks nodded. "Yeah." He lit his own cigarette and blew downward towards the muddy, dirty floor. The Marshal's face turned towards Cleve. "Don't blame yourself, Cleve. He had it coming — and more. You know that the woman — his wife, I understand — is dead, too, don't you?"

Cleve nodded, smoking in silence. He had a forlorn, hollow feeling that went with his listlessness and apathy. Death seemed to stalk in his footsteps. The incongruity of it all seemed to swell up within him as he sat puffing on his cigarette. How could order evolve from death, and peace grow out of war? Killings had come — and in the name of order, too — but they had been killings none the less.

The old house was silent as a tomb, then a posseman poked his head in the door, shot them both curious glances, and spoke to the Marshal. "You want us to start out now — pack Willis into town, Marshal?"

Hendricks nodded absently, looking a little

past the man. "I reckon. We'll catch up. Let somebody ride my horse, will you — and leave the top-buggy?"

The man nodded, hesitated, then spoke through a wry smile. "Sure thing, Marshal. Just leave the buggy at the courthouse, will you?"

Cleve looked up, saw the good-humoured line around the man's mouth, and spoke. "Willis took the buggy, pardner, but I took that extra horse out there. You reckon the man that owns —"

"Don't worry," the stranger said with an infectious grin. "Paddy O'Rourke owns that horse. He's downstairs, too. Helped carry this Willis hombre out. He's glad you took his critter — said so himself."

Cleve returned the smile. "Thanks, neighbour. Tell Paddy thanks for me, too, will you?"

"Sure; you bet." The pleasant eyes swung to Hendricks again. "We'll see you in town, Marshal?"

"Yes; we'll be along in a few minutes."

After the posse had wound its damp way down the lane, only the dull sound of sluggish water dripping from the ancient eaves broke in upon the silence.

Then Hendricks pressed out his cigarette and pushed off the wall. "Come on, Cleve;

175

I'll help you down to the buggy. We don't want to be gone too long. Your wife's worrying enough as it is."

Cleve looked up enquiringly. "Is she — she didn't — really think — I mean — that woman that got killed — she didn't think —"

Hendricks was watching Cleve stunned surprise. "Hell, no. Where'd you get that idea? Man, the last I saw of your wife, she was trying to borrow a pistol from a guard in the Legislature building so that she could chase after Willis, too." Hendricks bent over and offered Cleve an arm. "Commissioner Stevens said he'd keep her at the hotel until I — we — got back." A dull blush crept over the lawman's face.

Cleve felt better. He regarded the Marshal's arm with surprise, then scorn, and pushed himself erect. "Hell, I'm all right."

Hendricks watched him without answering, and wasn't the least bit surprised when Cleve walked halfway across the room and collapsed in a heap at the exact spot where Harold Willis had died. He helped the semi-conscious man to his feet and supported him down the stairs. He carried the man with a grunt over the wreckage where the chest had torn through the flimsy steps, and got him out to the buggy and into it, before he spoke.

"Sure; you're all right. There's nothing

wrong with you that about a week's sleep and a month's rest and some good Madeira served up by that handsome woman you're married to, won't be able to cure."

They drove back to Oregon City without speaking. Cleve was dully conscious that the road back to town was quite a bit rockier and bumpier than it had been on the way out.

At the courthouse, a large mob was gathered in the drizzle, white-faced and wide-eyed. Cleve had many hands help him from the top-buggy and into the hotel's lounge.

Then he felt Cathy's arm go around him and he turned to her. It was hard to tell whether all the moistness of her face was from the dreary drizzle, or if it was tears. He smiled and felt the surge of weak energy, the last of his inner reserve, flood through him.

"Honey — are you all right?" It sounded slightly ridiculous to his own ears when he said it.

Cathy looked a little startled. "Cleve, it's *you* that's hurt, honey — not me." She bent a little, reaching for the thick buffalo robe to wrap around him, tucking it firmly across his lap and upper body. The chore gave her a chance to hide the overpowering thankfulness she felt, that shone in her eyes and expression. A humble gratitude.

He felt small annoyance at the way she coddled him. "Cathy, don't, I'm all right."

Her face came up flushed with indignation. "You certainly are not! Do you want a chill? Then hold still, we'll be back at the hotel in a few minutes. I'll put you to bed."

"We can't stay here, honey; we've got to get back to Gold River. There's a lot to be —"

"There isn't a thing, Mister director-of-the-mint, that won't wait a week or ten days. Besides, this is our honeymoon, remember? I don't intend to be cheated out of it. The Lord knows whether we'd ever have had one if you hadn't been hurt. You're going to be a big man, Cleve Simpson, and I'm very thankful for that — but you'll also be a very busy man, and, therefore, we are going to have our honeymoon right now — here in Oregon City —"

He grinned at her. "It won't be much fun for you for a few days, dear."

She leaned across him, looked into his smoky grey eyes, and let the emotions that were raging within her show, unashamed, for the first time in her life. "Oh, yes, it will. I only want one thing for my honeymoon, Cleve — you!"

He kissed her, but when he closed his eyes the vision of Harold Willis's face floated slowly across his inner sight and he shook free, looking down at her sombrely. "Cathy, he's dead — I — I killed him."

The intense passion he had discovered in her, one that reminded him a little of Neila, flashed savagely across her face. "I'm glad, Cleve! Glad as — hell!"

Lauran Paine who, under his own name and various pseudonyms has written over 900 books, was born in Duluth, Minnesota, a descendant of the Revolutionary War patriot and author, Thomas Paine. His family moved to California when he was at an early age and his apprenticeship as a Western writer came about through the years he spent in the livestock trade, rodeos, and even motion pictures where he served as an extra because of his expert horsemanship in several films starring movie cowboy Johnny Mack Brown. In the late 1930s, Paine trapped wild horses in northern Arizona and even, for a time, worked as a professional farrier. Paine came to know the Old West through the eyes of many who had been born in the previous century and he learned that Western life had been very different from the way it was portrayed on the screen. "I knew men who had killed other men," he later recalled. "But they were the exceptions. Prior to and during the Depression, people were just too busy eking out an existence to indulge in Saturday-night brawls." He served in the U.S. Navy in the Second World War and began writing for Western pulp magazines following his discharge. It is interesting to note that all of his earliest novels (written under his own name and the pseudonym Mark Carrel) were published in the British market and he soon had as strong a following in that country as in the United States. Paine's Western fiction is characterized by strong plots, authenticity, an apparently effortless ability to construct situation and character, and a preference for building his stories upon a solid foundation of historical fact. ADOBE EMPIRE (1956), one of his best novels, is a fictionalized account of the last twenty years in the life of trader William Bent and, in an off-trail way, has a melancholy, bittersweet texture that is not easily forgotten. MOON PRAIRIE (1950), first published in the United States in 1994, is a memorable story set during the mountain man period of the frontier. In later novels such as THE HOMESTEADERS (1986) or THE OPEN RANGE MEN (1990), he showed that the special magic and power of his stories and characters had only matured along with his basic themes of changing times, changing attitudes, learning from experience, respecting nature, and the yearning for a simpler, more moderate way of life.

We hope you have enjoyed this Large Print book. Other Thorndike Press or Chivers Press Large Print books are available at your library or directly from the publishers. For more information about current and upcoming titles, please call or write, without obligation, to:

Thorndike Press
P.O. Box 159
Thorndike, Maine 04986
USA
Tel. (800) 223-6121
(207) 948-2962
(in Maine and Canada, call collect)

OR

Chivers Press Limited
Windsor Bridge Road
Bath BA2 3AX
England
Tel. (0225) 335336

All our Large Print titles are designed for easy reading, and all our books are made to last.